THE WORKS OF ANATOLE FRANCE
IN AN ENGLISH TRANSLATION
EDITED BY FREDERIC CHAPMAN

JOCASTA & THE FAMISHED CAT

JOCASTA & THE FAMISHED CAT

BY ANATOLE FRANCE

A TRANSLATION BY
AGNES FARLEY

LONDON: JOHN LANE, THE BODLEY HEAD
NEW YORK: JOHN LANE COMPANY
TORONTO: BELL & COCKBURN: MCMXII

NOTE

HEN, in 1879, Monsieur France published *Jocaste et Le Chat Maigre*, his first work of fiction, it contained a preface comprising a dedicatory letter addressed to Monsieur Charles Edmond and a story entitled *André*. The latter, when, in 1885, he put together his book, *Le Livre de mon Ami*, was transferred to the new volume. The former disappeared from the later editions of *Jocaste*. As nothing that comes from the great writer's pen can fail to interest, the dedicatory letter is here reproduced, with a word or two on the modifications introduced into the story on its introduction into its new environment. A translation of *André* will be found in its proper place in the translation by Mr. J. Lewis May of *Le Livre de mon Ami* which will follow closely upon the appearance of the present volume. The letter is as follows:—

DEAR SIR,—I should have liked to offer you some inspiring tale such as you yourself know so well how to present. *Jocaste*, which is what I bring for your acceptance, is steeped in violence and unrest. It is a sinister story, and even the best among the persons concerned in it are not altogether immaculate.

I have appended to it a little chronicle which we will, if you are agreeable, entitle *Le Chat Maigre*, and in which you will encounter none but the scatter-brained. One of the most gifted writers of the century once remarked to a sober-minded acquaintance, "No one who is sane affords me much amusement." May my lunatics bring with them to your fireside an hour's philosophical entertainment!

How much better inspired were you on that All Souls' Day when, in some hamlet in Alsace, you overtook an old forester and an elderly schoolmaster! They each of them bore a wreath which they set on a grave; and then, being alone in the world on that day of hallowed memories, beneath a gloomy storm-rent sky, they went off to sup together at the forester's hut.

You stole unawares into the secret recesses of their sturdy simplicity, and all that you record of their conversation is helpful and gives a feeling of that beatific refreshment—*dulce refrigerium*—which the early Christians invoke on their sepulchral marbles at Rome.

Your schoolmaster and forester, although disciplined by age and the labours of life, have yet unwittingly preserved tender hearts stored with joyous recollections. The poets tell us of hoary oaks whose hollows shelter swarms of bees so that their rugged rind drops honey. The memory of your worthy dominie is packed with touching and artless anecdotes. Above all about a little girl the mention of whom carries him outside himself and some of whose admirable sayings he quotes. I should like to chronicle one of them for the benefit of those who may read this letter after you.

"I set the little one on her feet again" (it is the schoolmaster who is speaking), "and hand in hand we resumed our way together. Something impelled me at the moment to confide to her the misfortune I had just sustained. 'No more holiday-making to-day, my pet,' I said to her finally; 'we are in mourning. My brother—you knew him well, he loved you dearly, he used to bring you toys—now he lies dead. He will be laid under the sod. Do not cry, my darling; it is only I who need cry. Yes, he is dead. But there! Each one in his turn! As to the *fête*, we will put it off till next year. You will lose nothing by waiting.' The child stopped short, and fixing her big terrified blue eyes on me said :

"'Next year, then, your brother will not be dead any longer?'"[1]

How this question, in its simple directness and sublime ignorance, pierces to our very marrow! At Bellevue there is a little creature, appropriately nick-named the Elephant, since no longer ago than last year she could have been hidden with ease in her godmother's muff, whose childish prattle is interspersed with utterances of as profound significance as this that you have so skilfully put on record.

A simple tale about a child has come to my ears which it would have gratified me to dedicate to you. But, alas, well as I am instructed as to its minutest details it will never be written by me. It would

---

[1] The day after All Saints' Day—(*Le lendemain de la Toussaint*) in the *Revue Alsacienne*, May 1878.

recall in more than one feature the delightful scenes at the Rookery at Blunderstone, and my characters, truthful as they might be, would grow pale and dwindle to vain shadows beside the ever charming inmates of Dickens' cottage. After all, since I am only talking to you just now, I can very well tell you this story that will never be written. Here it is.

The tale is about the charming widow of a clever young surgeon, sprung from the peasantry, and her little boy, André. The child, as he grows, loses flesh and colour, so his mother resolves for his sake to pay a visit to his grandparents in their humble little farmhouse, and mother and child are received with open arms, the child in particular making a complete conquest of the old folks. The best bed-room was allotted to the Parisian visitors, a room which the grandparents had never occupied since their bridal night.

At this point in the reprinted story the author has, for some reason, struck out the following paragraph :—

The two old people slept as they were accustomed to do in the downstairs room behind the curtain that hung from the beam of the staircase. Madame Trévière's nurse made her way timorously up a steep ladder into the attic, where she slept surrounded by onions.

The advent of the lovely young mother flutters the heart of a wealthy manufacturer, a patron of

Millet and the Barbizon school, Philippe Lassalle, and he pays assiduous court to her. Little André instinctively recognises the menace of the interloper and exerts all his potent influence against the success of Lassalle. One night, when the child is being put to bed, he says, "Mamma, I'm afraid." At this point again the author has cut out a few words, for in the earlier version André continues :—

"I like being afraid. It's nice. It's like swimming"—swimming being in his customary talk his most forcible description of a pleasant sensation.

This adoption of an expression for which he made a meaning of his own is so eminently childlike a touch that it seems a thousand pities to have cut out the passage.

The widow sits by the child's cot and muses over a letter in which Lassalle has asked her to marry him, when the child stirs in his sleep and inquires whether his dead father can come back again. Being told no, he declares that he is glad because he loves his mother so much that he has no love left over for his father if he should come back.

The mother soothes him, saying, "Sleep on ; he will not come back."

And then, perhaps desirous that the tale should not too closely resemble the chronicle of the early troubles of David Copperfield, Monsieur France closed his story thus :—

He will not come back. Monsieur Lassalle no longer nurses any hope. His appeal has met with a rebuff. Of an evening in his room hung with landscapes and bits of still-life, with his feet on the bars, as he fills his pipe and mixes his grog, he reflects that winter evenings are sufficiently gloomy when one sits alone. He has not seen the widow since; but when his friends ask him what has become of her, he answers bravely in a cheerful tone that disguises his profound disappointment, "She is still the beautiful Madame Trévière : more so than ever."

In fitting the tale into *Le Livre de mon Ami*, however, the author found a way to remove the widow's scruples without hinting at any Murdstone-like proclivities on the part of Monsieur Lassalle. In the later version the story ends thus :—

Nevertheless, when two months were over, he did come back, and he came back with the broad, sun-burnt features of Monsieur Lassalle, the new master of the house. And little André began to grow sallow and thin and listless.

He is cured again now. He loves his nurse with the love he used to bestow on his mother; but he doesn't know his nurse has got a young man.

The letter to Monsieur Edmond is then resumed as follows :—

There, in a few strokes, is the tale I shall never write. It is true. Accept, in default of better, the tales I *have* written, I hardly know how, or why. The narrator is like that inamorata of the old poet

Mellin de Sainct-Gelais who had more moons in her head [1] than there are gondolas at Venice. I most certainly had a red moon [2] in my brain when I recast from unimpeachable materials the narrative which owes its title, *Jocaste*, to a circumstance as simple as it is singular. As for the moon that "governed" the *Chat Maigre*, it was the one that rises ruddily over the roofs of Paris. About this last there is nothing either mysterious or terrible. I beg you to accept these two tales as a feeble testimony of my gratitude and affection. A. F.

---

[1] *Avoir la lune dans la tête*=To be a little mad.—LITTRÉ.

The use of a corresponding idiom is rendered impracticable by the author's subsequent play upon the word *lune*.

[2] *Lune rousse*=The April moon, which gardeners assert turns young leaves and buds red: the effects it is said to produce are attributable to a nocturnal fall in the temperature.—LITTRÉ.

CONTENTS

JOCASTA

JOCASTA

CHAPTER I

WHAT! Monsieur Longuemare, you put live frogs into your pocket? How disgusting!"

"When I get back to my room Mademoiselle, I shall nail one of them on a small board and lay bare his mesentery, having first excited it with a pair of delicate pincers."

"But the poor frog will endure tortures."

"That depends. It would suffer more, for instance, in the summer than in the winter. And if its mesentery should be inflamed, perhaps, because of some anterior lesion, the pain would be so intense that its heart would cease to beat."

"What good can it do you to hurt an animal like that?"

"It helps me to construct my experimental theory of pain. I shall prove that the Stoics did not know what they were talking about, and that Zeno was an idiot. You don't know who Zeno was? Well,

don't seek to make his acquaintance. He denied
the reality of sensation, whereas I maintain that
sensation is everything. You will possess an exact
and sufficient notion of the Stoics when I tell you
they were dull maniacs, who affectedly pretended to
despise suffering. If I had one of the barbarians
under my tweezers in the place of my frog, he
would quickly find out if one can suppress suffering
by an effort of the will. Besides, it is a good thing
for living beings to be endowed with the faculty for
suffering."

"You must be joking. In what way can it be
good to be able to suffer?"

"It is a necessary safeguard. If, for example, the
flames did not scorch us intolerably when we go too
near the fire, we should be roasted to the bone
without knowing it."

He gazed at her.

"And," he added, after a moment, "pain is
beautiful. Richet says, 'There is such a strong
affinity between intelligence and suffering, that the
most intelligent beings are the most susceptible to
pain.'"

"So naturally you think you are more capable of
suffering than any one else. I would ask you to
describe your sufferings to me, if I were not afraid
of being indiscreet."

"I have already told you, Mademoiselle, that

Zeno was a fool. If I were in great pain I should scream. As for you, you have a most delicate organisation—your nerves are like sensitive strings; you present pain with a sonorous instrument, an eight octave keyboard on which it could play, if it chose, the most elaborate and complicated variations."

"Which in plain language means I am to be very unhappy. You are insupportable; one never knows if you are speaking seriously or not. And your ideas are so extraordinary that the little I understand of them makes me giddy. Will you answer me properly and sensibly, if you can, for once in your life? Is it true that you are leaving us and going very far away?"

"Yes, Mademoiselle, it is true. I have bidden an eternal farewell to Val de Grâce.[1] I shall prescribe no more cooling draughts for the patients there. It is by my own request that I have been removed from the hospital staff and appointed assistant doctor in Cochin-China. I made up my mind on this point, as I do on all others, after most mature reflexion—you smile, you think I am frivolous. I will tell you my reasons for leaving France. First and foremost, I shall escape the tyranny of *concierges*, charwomen, landladies, waiters, old-clothes men, and all such inveterate enemies of domestic happiness. I shall

[1] The military hospital in Paris.

no longer have to bear with the smile of the
café waiter—by-the-bye, have you noticed that
waiters always have magnificently shaped heads?
This is a very acute observation, but it would
be useless to develop to you the theories it
suggests.   I am going far from the Boulevard
Saint-Michel, but I shall find at Shanghai osteo-
logical monuments which will enable me to finish
my treatise on the dentition of the yellow races.
I shall lose that bright colour, which according to
you is the proof of insolent good health, and take
on the more interesting appearance of a lemon whose
days are numbered.   I shall develop complicated
disorders of the liver, and study them with lively
curiosity.   You must own that all this is worth the
voyage?"

Thus spoke René Longuemare, assistant surgeon
of the First Division, standing in a suburban garden
that surrounded a small chalet.   Before him was a
lawn, a fountain with an artificial grotto, a Judas-
tree, and holly bushes growing against the railings;
beyond the garden, in the distance, lay the beautiful
valley, with the Seine winding on the left between
pale green banks, crossed on the right by the white
line of an aqueduct, and disappearing into that
immensity of roofs, steeples, and domes which is
Paris.   In the hazy distance the gilded rotunda of
the Invalides flung back the rays of sunlight.   It

was a warm, blue day in July; a few little white clouds hung motionless in the sky.

The girl to whom René Longuemare was speaking sat in an iron garden-chair. She raised her great clear eyes to the young surgeon's face, but remained silent—a somewhat sad, uncertain expression on her lips.

Her eyes, of an indefinite colour, were timid, but at the same time so languorous that the whole face they illuminated acquired a singular expression of sensuousness, though her nose was straight and her cheeks slightly hollow.

She was so uniformly pale that other women in speaking of her were wont to say, "The girl has no complexion." Her mouth was too large and somewhat flaccid, but showed facility and benevolent instincts.

René Longuemare, with a visible effort, recommenced his detestable joking.

"No," he said; "I must own up, Mademoiselle; in leaving France I am running away from my bootmaker. I can't stand his German accent any longer."

She asked him again if he was really going. He ceased smiling abruptly, and said:

"I am taking the train to-morrow morning, at seven fifty-five, and on the twenty-sixth I go aboard the steamship *Magenta* at Toulon."

He could hear the sound of the ivory billiard

balls clicking against each other on the table, and from the chalet came a voice, with a strong southern intonation, proclaiming emphatically :

"Seven, fourteen."

He flung a hurried look through the glass doors at the players, frowned, and with a somewhat brusque farewell to the young girl, turned swiftly away, his face distorted and his eyes brimming with tears. The girl saw him thus for a moment in profile above the holly hedge, behind the iron lances of the railings. She rose and ran to the gate, her handkerchief pressed to her mouth as though to stifle a cry ; then resolutely she stretched out her arms and called in a strangled voice :

" René ! "

Her arms dropped to her side ; it was too late, he did not hear.

She leaned her head against an iron bar. Her drawn features, the abandonment of her whole being, showed irreparable defeat. The southern voice called from the chalet :

"Hélène ! the madeira."

It was Monsieur Fellaire de Sisac calling to his daughter. He was standing, his little figure drawn up to its full height before the board on which the billiard players marked their score by means of wooden rings strung on wires. With a wide, magnifient gesture he rubbed the end of his cue with chalk, his eyes sparkled beneath their thick bushy brows. He looked capable and well satisfied, although he had just been badly beaten at the game.

"Mr. Haviland," he said to his guest, "I am particularly anxious that my daughter herself should do us the honours of my madeira. I am like that, you see, patriarchal and biblical. Being an islander, I think you are especially qualified to appreciate good wine in general, and madeira in particular. Taste this, I beg you."

Mr. Haviland turned his dull eyes on Hélène and silently took the glass she offered him on a lacquered tray. He was a long personage, with long teeth and long feet—carroty, bald, and dressed in checked clothes. He wore a racing glass slung from his shoulder by a strap.

Hélène disappeared. She had looked at her father uneasily. She had appeared disturbed at hearing him pour forth his voluble politenesses. She sent word to say she was not feeling well, and wished to be excused appearing at dinner.

Monsieur Fellaire de Sisac filled the dining-room, which was painted like a boulevard café, with his noisy presence, fussily carving, passing dishes, pouring out wine, calling in loud tones for the fish-slice when it was just under his eyes, trying the edge of the knife with the gravity of a charlatan at a fair, and tucking his serviette high up in his waistcoat. He boasted of his wines, and talked for ten minutes about a certain dry syracuse before uncorking it.

The gardener, a type of the suburban peasant hired by the year, waited at table. He was a sly, malicious-looking creature, who answered back when his master spoke to him, although the latter pretended not to notice his impertinence.

Mr. Haviland, a high-coloured, florid man, ate a great deal, became very red in the face, but did not change his melancholy expression, and hardly spoke.

Fellaire de Sisac, after declaring that he did not intend to talk about business, proceeded to expatiate on his principal operations. He was a commission agent, and found his clients mostly among landlords and shopkeepers whose property had been expropriated. The new streets and boulevards which were being so rapidly opened up by Monsieur Haussmann gave him plenty to do.

He must, as a matter of fact, have made a good deal of money in a short time (although he did not say so). For many years he was to be seen daily, with a portfolio under his arm, dragging his down-at-heel boots about the neighbourhood of the Rue Rambuteau. There in a dingy office at the end of a courtyard he held consultations with sundry pork-butchers in distress.

It was in this unhealthy place that he developed

the pale, puffy cheeks which thenceforth hung down on either side of his face.

On the brass plate affixed to his door his name appeared first as " Fellaire," followed by the words " de Sisac" in parenthesis, as indicating his birthplace :—

" Fellaire (de Sisac)."

On a new plate above the threshold of a new domicile, the parenthesis was replaced by a comma after the first name :—

" Fellaire, de Sisac."

On a third plate, put up after a third removal, the comma was suppressed, and there was nothing to indicate its having once existed :—

" Fellaire de Sisac."

Now there was no plate on the commission agent's door. He occupied, when in town, an apartment ornamented with much looking-glass, on the first floor of a house in the Rue Neuve des Petits Champs ; besides which he built for himself, as a country residence, the chalet at Meudon.

Monsieur Fellaire was a native of Sisac, near Saint-Mamet-la-Salvétat, in the department of Cantal, where his brother, the miller, still lived.

When Fellaire de Sisac learnt that a portion of that part of Paris, known as the Butte-des-Moulins

or Windmill Hill, had to come down, so as to open
up the approach to the Théâtre Français, he sent
out cards, prospectuses, and circulars, and made
visits to the owners and principal tradespeople of
the condemned houses.   On one of what he spoke
of as his "rounds" he called on Mr. Haviland,
who lived at the Hôtel Meurice, and was the
proprietor of a large house situated at the foot of
the Butte, near the theatre.   This house had belonged to the Haviland family for nearly two
centuries.

John Haviland, the banker, established offices
there in 1789.   He had placed considerable sums
of money at the disposition of the Duke of Orleans,
who would, he considered, surely succeed Louis
XVI. if the French were, as he thought, tending
towards a constitutional monarchy.   But the plans
of the ambitious banker were not furthered either
by the violent march of events or by the naturally
wavering duke, who went back to the royal cause
and favoured the counter-revolution.

Haviland then put himself in communication
with the queen through the intervention of the
beautiful Mrs. Elliot, but on the tenth of August,
after the definite fall of royalty, he was obliged
to fly to England, though he remained in communication with the Duke of Brunswick and the
princes.   His cashier, David Ewart, a man then

eighty-one years of age, insisted on remaining in Paris to look after the threatened interests of the bank. Not having been able to obtain a certificate of citizenship, and so looked on as " suspect," he was arrested and taken to the Conciergerie, where for over four months he seemed to be forgotten. Finally, on the 1st Thermidor 1794, he was haled before the revolutionary tribunal, which condemned him to capital punishment as a conspirator, and he was guillotined the same day at the Barrière du Trône, then called the Barrière Renversée.

Haviland's bank was saved from ruin by the energetic fidelity of this old man, but the house on the Butte-des-Moulins ceased to be one of its branches, and was let for other purposes.

It was very black and dirty when marked for the pickaxe. The windows to the front were surmounted by the Louis XV. shell, and a head wearing a helmet still grimaced heroically above the keystone of the arch of the courtyard door; but it was squeezed between the mural signs of a dyer and cleaner and a locksmith, and was painted blue on one side and yellow on the other. To the right and left of the door, and under the archway, hung little boards displaying the names of copyists and dressmakers. Within, the stone staircase, with its magnificent balluster of wrought iron, was befouled with dust, spittle, and dead salad leaves, and per-

meated by an acrid alkaline smell. The squalling
of children was audible on the landings, and through
the half-open doors could be seen women in bed-
gowns and men in shirt-sleeves, the undress of the
worker or the loafer.

Such was the Haviland house in its last days.

Monsieur Fellaire de Sisac, being entrusted with
the interests of the owner, visited it. He noted
that it possessed thirty yards of frontage, two
shops with offices and dependencies, and afforded
shelter besides to thirty-two trading enterprises
of divers sorts, with their appurtenances, including
a female costermonger who kept her barrow in the
coach-house, and a sempstress who stitched at a
sewing-machine in the garret.

A detailed account of the whole was given in a
report destined to impress a due sense of its immense
value on the Council of Indemnities, appointed by the
city to satisfy expropriated landlords. If, as was
not unlikely, the affair should come before a com-
petent tribunal, de Sisac was to arrange with barrister
and lawyer.

He invited Haviland to dine with him first in
Paris and afterwards at Meudon; for he was hospit-
able to all his clients, partly from inclination, partly
from policy. He could manage men better from
behind a decanter, and became most persuasive at
dessert. He was convivial, and liked opening bottles.

"This is life," he would say. In the less prosperous epochs of his existence he treated his customers to roast chestnuts and white wine on the oilcloth covered tables of some small café. This was in the days of consultations with embarrassed shopkeepers. Now he received his clients in his own house, with his own silver and linen marked with his initials.

The last red rays of the setting sun lighted up the dining-room of the chalet where Haviland and de Sisac sat over their coffee, the business man with his pendulous cheeks was watching his guest narrowly.

"Just try this brandy, dear islander," he said.

The appellation *insulaire* seemed to him an elegant synonym for Englishman. He would sometimes speak of Albion instead of England, though he admitted that this was a little romantic.

Haviland drank the brandy, asked for a glass of wine, and then said :

"I hope that Mademoiselle Fellaire is not seriously indisposed?"

De Sisac said he hoped so also, and Haviland relapsed into his usual silence.

At last he rose with an English awkwardness accentuated by arthritis, for his knees were crippled with this rheumatic affliction. With his yellow overcoat over his arm, he had already passed through the garden gate, when he spoke again.

"I have the honour," he said to his host, "to ask

you for the hand of your daughter, Mademoiselle Fellaire."

The little man was probably about to make some adroit but petulant reply, when the Englishman put a paper into his hand.

"You will find there," he said, "an exact account of my fortune. Let me have your answer by registered letter, please. Do not accompany me any farther. No."

And he walked off stiffly towards the railway station.

Fellaire though not easily surprised, was startled. He trotted at a sprightly pace twelve times round the fountain before he could recover his composure, the moon shining on his fat inert face gave it the appearance of a mask.

"What?" he said; "this man who is no more to me than the two hundred other strangers I come into contact with in the course of the year; this man who has seen my daughter perhaps half-a-dozen times, and who scarcely opens his mouth, opens it now to make her a proposal of marriage! I wonder if it is Hélène who has arranged this little comedy for two actors so deftly? But no, I'm no fool; I know what is going on in my own house, and I don't believe the poor child has spoken more than four words to him. I'm afraid she will not receive this proposition as she ought to."

He stood still, biting his thumb, gazing fixedly
ahead like a man measuring some obstacle; then
he turned deliberately back to the chalet. He
stopped in the dining-room and read the paper
Haviland had given him, before going upstairs to
his daughter's room. He put his cigar down on
the pink chintz of the mantelpiece, and drew a chair
to the bedside. He might have been the family
doctor as he asked :

"Well, and how are we now, my pet ? "

As she did not answer, he added :

"Mr. Haviland inquired after you this evening
in the most affectionate manner."

Then, after a pause, he went on in the unctuous
voice of a man who has dined well.

"What do you think of him ? "

No answer came to his question, but by the light of
the candle burning on the mantelpiece he could see
her eyes were open and staring, her brows contracted
with an air of painful reflexion. He judged rightly
that she had guessed Haviland's intentions, and no
longer afraid of striking too sudden a blow, said :

"Mr. Haviland has made you an offer of
marriage."

"I don't want to marry; I am quite happy with
you."

He settled himself more comfortably in the easy-
chair, arranged his hands on his knees, drew a

whistling breath through his throat, husky with spirits but soothed with sweetmeats, and said in a businesslike tone :

"You don't ask me what my answer was, little girl?"

"Well, what was it?"

"My child, I said nothing which could in any way bind you. I want to leave you entirely free. I don't consider that I have a right to impose my will on you. You know well enough I'm no tyrant."

She sat up, her elbow on the pillow.

"No, you are a dear father, and if I don't want to be married you won't force me to be."

"I tell you again, child," he said good-naturedly, "you are as free as air, but we can discuss these little matters. I am your father, I love you, and there are lots of things you are old enough now to understand. Come, let's talk like a pair of friends. We live together, you and I, and we live very comfortably; but we have not got what could be called a settled fortune. I am a self-made man, and success came to me late—too late. Much water will flow under the bridge before I can provide a dowry for you; and between this and then, who knows what may happen? You are twenty-two, and the offer you have had to-day is not to be despised. It is an extraordinary piece of luck, if I may say so. Haviland is not what one would call a young man. You see, my girl, I am quite impartial; but he is a gentleman, a real gentleman. He is very rich."

With his mouth full, as it were, of this last word, he slapped the pocket in which was the paper the Englishman had given him, and went on, warming to the subject:

"This devil of a Haviland has the command of a magnificent fortune—houses, forests, farms, stocks and shares, everything."

She shrugged her shoulders with a disgusted look, and he saw he had put things rather too brutally.

"Don't imagine, child, that I want you to marry for money as they say; no, I love you and I only want you to be happy."

He really did love his daughter, and paternal affection made his voice tremble.

"God is my witness that I only want your happiness. I know what sentiment is; when I married your mother she hadn't a penny. To tell you the truth I am really a dreamer, a sentimentalist. I am very romantic at bottom. Do you know what I should have liked better than anything, if circumstances had permitted?—to live in the country and write poetry! But there, I was caught, body and soul, by business. Now I am dragged into it up to my neck. Good Lord! life isn't all rose-coloured, one has to make certain sacrifices. Well, well, my girl, my dream has always been to spare you such sacrifices, to shield you from the troubles and miseries of existence. It is enough that your poor mother should have had to endure them, and die at the task—die at the task! Do you hear me?"

He wiped his eyes with the back of his hand, much moved by the memory he had conjured up— as a matter of fact, his wife died of consumption at Niort, where her family lived, and where he had sent her to be out of the way; but he was intoxicated and maudlin with his own eloquence. He took his daughter's face between his hands, covered it with kisses and burst forth again:

"Listen to me, my Lili. I know you, and I know you *must* have comfort, luxury even. It is my fault. I have been too ambitious. Nothing was too good or too fine for you. I have brought you up as a rich man's child. You haven't learnt how to wait on yourself or to keep accounts. If you are not well off you will surely be the most miserable of women, and it will be my fault. What a responsibility for your poor father! I should die of it. But here is Fortune knocking at your door, hey? Little girl, shall we let her in? See now; I love you—I adore you, my darling, but I know what is best for you. Love is never deceived. Let me settle this."

Hélène asked in a careless tone if Mr. Haviland intended to live in Paris.

"Yes, certainly," answered de Sisac, though he knew nothing whatever of Haviland's plans. He added that his future son-in-law had elegant manners, and was still capable of turning the head of many a young woman. As to his feelings, they were most delicate, . . . it was difficult to imagine any one with such delicate feelings. Finally, as a last resource, he spoke of an hotel, carriages, and jewels.

Hélène was thinking that René Longuemare had gone, far away and for a long time, without a word of love, without a word of regret. If he had only said he would come back, that he would think of her—remember her. But no, he had said nothing. Evidently, then, he did not care for her. He only cared for his books, his phials, his scalpels, and his tweezers. He had liked her because she had been so willing to listen to him, that was all. He had said a thousand silly things to her, as he would to any girl. But supposing he cared for her secretly, as she had often thought? Well, it would be a just revenge for his desertion. What her father said was true; she was made to be rich, she had a vocation for the luxurious life. And how could she resist? She was too tired to struggle; the first assault had overthrown her, and her father would return to the charge.

Hers was one of those souls which accept defeat in advance. Then, too, the love of this foreigner was flattering. She knew from certain indications how true and profound that love was : this man who was verging on the decline of life, who for twenty-five years had travelled all over the world without being able to dissipate his eternal *ennui;* this man, glacial towards every one else, had caught fire like a young man—he had known her for three months, and his visits to her had been almost silent, yet he offered her his hand and fortune; was he not strange, chivalrous, generous? Would it not be possible to love him! She raised her pretty face, with its undecided expression, towards her father and murmured:

"We will see."

CHAPTER II

ÉLÈNE FELLAIRE had been brought up, in many respects, as a rich man's daughter. It is true she could remember periods in her childhood when her stockings were in holes, when her feet were often cold, and the food seemed to consist principally of plates of sausage from the cook-shop, which she particularly detested; when she had to spend long hours waiting in courtyards and doorways while one of the many removals of their household goods was in progress, when in the winter evenings her mother's face grew downcast.

When she thought of her mother, it was of some one who was always singing or scolding, restlessly active, or completely broken down; some one who was always tormented or tormenting.

One of her recollections was of their travelling together, where to or exactly at what time she could not recall, but it was when she was very young. One night her mother, having put her to bed, turned her face to the wall and sternly told her

to go to sleep. Then the poor lady took off her
chemise and washed it in the basin. It amused
Hélène immensely to see her mother, rolled up in a
shawl, busy among the soap-suds. Later on, when
she understood that it was because they were too
poor to pay a washerwoman, she felt frightened.

She was an affectionate, delicate creature from
her infancy. Her heart would melt at the sight
of suffering. She gave sweets and doll's clothes
to poor children. She kept a sparrow in a cage
and stuffed it with sugar; it was a source of joy
and sorrow to her, for one day it perished miserably,
crushed to death by a door.

"Praxo raised a tomb to her grasshopper, by
whose death she learnt that all things must die."

Thus the poet of The Anthology makes the
Ionian child speak.

The loss of the sparrow filled Hélène with a
terror of death which did not leave her for many
years.

Her father was a man with a winning tongue.
He spent his money lavishly, and stayed out late
at night, so that his wife, faded by poverty and
ceaselessly shaken by jealousy, could not possess
that quiet and peace of mind, that constant, watchful
foresight parents need to enable them to direct
skilfully and happily the appealing little souls they
have brought into the world; so Hélène, hugged

or smacked without knowing why, grew dull and stupid, and gave up trying to distinguish between right and wrong.

"This child will be the death of me!" Madame Fellaire would exclaim. "I don't know what I have done that God should have afflicted me with such a monster."

Then would follow a storm of vociferations, accompanied by sobs, clenched fists, and banging doors. The poor child used to creep away to bed and cry herself to sleep with a heavy heart. When morning came she would often be awakened by a shower of kisses, gentle words, and pretty little songs; her mother's mood having been changed and brightened by a few tardy attentions from Monsieur Fellaire.

As for him, to Hélène's mind he always appeared very handsome, very good, and very grand. His thick whiskers and his white waistcoats were marvels of elegance to her. Monsieur Fellaire was a god in his daughter's eyes, but after the manner of gods, showed himself rarely. He was away all day, and came home late. Sometimes, when things outside went against him, he would have bursts of domestic assiduity. On such occasions he would take his Lili driving, or to the Zoological Gardens, or to a café, where she drank sugared water and even syrups. She would dip the end of her tongue in

her father's glass and grimace at the bitter taste
of the green beverage. Such outings were delicious,
but infrequent. The god faded away, leaving his
wife more sullen and more irritable than before,
and Hélène, sitting by her in her little chair, would
dream lovingly of him and recall the dazzling
vision of his wonderful white waistcoat; she was
lazy, and happiest doing nothing, an occupation in
which she succeeded best of all. Madame Fellaire
never noticed the long silent reveries of her
daughter, but a peal of infantine laughter would
make her break out in reproaches.

Hélène was keenly and precociously alive to
sensation. She instinctively loved luxury, and did
what she could to improve the paternal ordinary.
Her liking for the delicacies of the table and the
refinements of dress delighted Monsieur Fellaire, who
was a connoisseur on both points.

She was seven years old when he put her to school
at Auteuil, at the Convent of the Ladies of Mount
Calvary. The white dresses and the white faces of
the Mothers, the peacefulness of the house and the
unfailingly regular life, did her much good.

One day she was told that her mother, who
had gone on a journey, would never return again.
This "never again" frightened her—she sobbed
bitterly. They dressed her in a black pinafore,
and let her run loose in the garden. The garden

was for her an immense mysterious country, full of living things—an enchanted world, a land of miracles. Her father came to see her there every week, and brought her cakes; his love and fatherly pride were most admirable.

Tired as he was with uselessly tramping the pavements, with climbing painfully up and down stairs, knocking at doors only to have them shut in his face; of writing his letters on the corner of some dirty café table; of following up chance clients, sometimes even to the suburban balls they frequented, where he would treat them to a bowl of mulled wine ; nosing like a hound after pettifogging law disputes, he would appear every Thursday in the parlour of the Ladies of Calvary, brushed up, shining, gloved, freshly shaved, and with immaculate linen. There he showed only as a being happy and at ease. His fat white cheeks were most presentable. Mother Sainte-Geneviève, the superior of the house at Auteuil, showed him much consideration. Two of the elder girls dreamt of him at night.

Hélène admired him immensely.

Truly, Monsieur Fellaire was heroic in his own fashion. One day, when he had not a penny in his pocket, he saw the poems of Alfred de Musset on a friend's table and promptly borrowed the volume. "I want to re-read it for the hundredth time," he said, and went off and sold it on the *quais*, so as to buy the gloves he drew on carelessly next day, under the watchful eyes of the sister doorkeeper.

The cakes he took for Hélène and her friends on his weekly visits came from a celebrated pastry-cook's, and the sweets were in most tasteful boxes full of mottoes and surprises. Mother Sainte-Geneviève, having conceived a great esteem for him, consulted him one day on some litigious matter. He gladly placed his time, his activity, and his knowledge at her disposal. She deigned to accept them. He was radiant with joy and pride. Such was his desire to please, that he tied up his notes and papers with blue ribbon, and managed to treat even legal matters with a degree of unction. When he ran through these documents with the Reverend Mother, he moistened his thumb with the tip of his tongue in a discreet and modest manner. As a matter of fact, each consultation was torture to him, but it was a delicious torture. He would listen for hours together to the explanations of the good lady, who was at once narrow-minded, mistrustful, obstinate, and gentle, and who promptly slipped out of everything with an ease born of long practice. She was a fine fair woman, a little puffy perhaps, and kept her eyes cast down and her hands in her sleeves, and spoke in a low voice. These manners intimidated him. He was more at ease with his usual clients, suburban publicans and manufacturers of patent hygienic belts, who would fling a bundle of judgment orders and summonses down on his roll-top desk, swearing horribly the while.

Mother Sainte-Geneviève had the grand manners of an abbess of the old régime. One of her affected elegances was to ignore the fact that Fellaire could ever need money. He was constantly called on to make advances to the Community, to obtain even the smallest of which involved strategy which would have turned an ordinary brain. But what a pleasure it was for him to go to Vespers on Sunday and sit in the gallery of the chapel, which smelt of incense and orris root, and from his place he could see his daughter in the aisle, bending over her prayer-book, seated between the daughter of a councillor of State and the cousin of a Montenegrin prince! After contemplating her pretty hair, and her shoulders, a little thin and pointed in her brown merino bodice, the glasses of his spectacles would grow misty, and he would blow his nose as one does at the theatre after a moving scene. The business of the Community cost him some money, but brought him many useful acquaintances.

"I am becoming the fashion," he said to himself, and his chest would swell with renewed ampleness beneath his fancy waistcoat, of white piqué, or printed, stamped, or spotted velvet.

As Hélène grew up, she grew beautiful. Her
hair which for a long time had been like her
mother's, pale and faded, turned to a magnificent
gold. She was gentle, slothful, easily discouraged,
given to bursts of affection and sudden emotions.
It was with difficulty they could coax her to eat anything in the refectory beyond salad and bread and
salt. She had a friend, Cécile, at whose house she
spent the half-holidays. This friend, the daughter
of a stockbroker, was a little person of sixteen, at
once childish, old-fashioned, and coquettish, neither
ill-natured nor mischievous, too unimaginative to be
vicious, and very rich. She had the mind of a
dull woman of thirty, and her companions endowed her with an extraordinary prestige. She
had a heavily upholstered bedroom in her father's
house at Passy, and here she and Hélène would
pass hours eating bonbons. When the latter left
this stuffy nest, something in her soul had withered,
the outside world seemed duller, harder, and more
repulsive—her spirits flagged. Her day-dream was
to have a blue bedroom and to lie on a sofa
reading novels all day long. She developed pains
in her chest which quite pulled her down. One
night there was a wild scare in the convent. At
the cry of "Fire! fire!" all the girls jumped out
of bed and, rolled in blankets and petticoats, rushed
pell-mell down the staircase. The little ones came

last, with outstretched arms, shrieking and stumbling in their long night-dresses. It was soon discovered to be merely a false alarm. Mother Sainte-Geneviève scolded the foolish creatures and congratulated Hélène on having had the good sense not to leave her bed. If she had not moved, it was from pure inertia and the species of cowardice with which she faced every incident of life. Things slipped by her, leaving her indifferent to her surroundings; she thought of nothing but dresses, jewels, horses, and boating excursions. She would burst into tears at the mention of her father's name.

She left the convent knowing how to enter a drawing-room and play a waltz on the piano. She found the paternal house completely refurnished; she was to do the honours of it, and she had her blue bedroom.

Her father treated her with the kindness and liberality of an old lover for a young mistress. He took her to the little theatres, and to supper after the play. He thought this was the right thing to do. It was a cruel awakening for her when she discovered that this good, easy father was not the perfect gentleman she had supposed him to be in the convent parlour. His manners, which were a mixture of those of a quack doctor and a commercial traveller, wounded her terribly. She had learnt good behaviour with the Ladies of Mount

Calvary, and knew instinctively what was right and proper.

Her beauty attracted men, but their vivacious admiration only roused her indignation. Not one among them proposed to marry her; they all resembled each other, and were all alike stupid and tiresome. Uneasy, affected, feverish, nail-biting creatures, they one and all seemed possessed with the desire to wear out their boots, their horses, and their lives as quickly as possible. Then came some one who interested her.

A young army surgeon, René Longuemare. He had been sent by his father, a road surveyor in the Ardennes, to consult Fellaire de Sisac on some matter of business; he returned again and again to the house in the Rue Neuve des Petits Champs and became a constant visitor there.

Although he was not handsome, being clumsily built, with a high-coloured face, and although his conversation was rough and obscure, Hélène liked to see him, and to hear him talk. He would hold forth on matters of religion and morality in a way which made her hair stand on end, but which amused her, though she but half understood what he said.

"Man is descended from a monkey," he would say.

When she protested, he would develop his thesis in a way at once bold and comical.

Longuemare introduced some of his friends, and so a circle of young savants was formed in the house of the good Fellaire, who paid not the slightest attention to them.

The surgeon would advance theories like the following :—

"Virtue is a product, the same as phosphorus or vitriol."

"Heroism and holiness are the results of congestion of the brain."

"General paralysis is the only thing which makes a great man."

"The gods are adjectives."

"Things have always existed and will always exist."

"How wicked of you!" she would say.

But she took pleasure in listening to the manly young voice. She admired, as a mysterious force, the free and expansive intelligence which, of an evening, between a cup of tea and a glass of kirsch, would fling pell-mell before her the eccentricity, the magnificence, and the horror of Nature, as a barbarian flings his tribute at the feet of a surprised and flattered queen. Meanwhile, from the salon came the murmur of doleful voices talking of unpaid notes of hand, of decisions of the Chamber of Commerce and disputed building accounts.

Then came a shadow, wandering silently among

the divers groups—a big, stiff, red-headed shadow,
at once grotesque and noble. It was the troubled
soul of Mr. Haviland. Hélène never confounded
him with the others; she recognised that he possessed a certain nobility and distinction of mind,
and she knew that he loved her, although he never
spoke to her.

As for Longuemare, he was naïf, in spite of his
scientific audacity ; he respected her profoundly, and
admired her in silence. After having made some
great show of brutality, he would talk to her in
the most gentle and delicate way. He was always
gay in her presence, partly because it was his nature,
and partly from strength of will, for he loved her ;
and rather than tell her so, he would have bitten
his tongue through. He had only his pay, while
waiting for something better to turn up. He
never doubted but that Mademoiselle Fellaire was
rich. She used to tease him, and pretend to believe that he was frivolous, and even worse ; but
she was becoming strongly and profoundly attached
to him, until the day when he came to Meudon to
bid her a brusque farewell.

CHAPTER III

THE house on the Butte-des-Moulins had fallen; the mask with its one blue and one yellow cheek had crumbled beneath the pickaxe. The little room where the old cashier David Ewart was arrested, to be taken to the revolutionary tribunal and the guillotine, had gone with the rest. For some time clouds of grey dust rose from the ruins and whirled about the neighbouring streets, carrying particles of the old dwelling down the throats of men and horses. Now those who had inhabited it—the dyer and cleaner and the locksmith among others—could not have exactly indicated the spot where it had stood.

The domain of Monsieur Fellaire de Sisac at Meudon had grown considerably larger. The railings which formerly were quite near the house had retreated so as to take in a piece of neighbouring land, on which immediately sprang up a summer-house built like a Gothic château, with towers, battlements, and portcullis in brick. The property was entitled the Villa de Sisac. The plaster was still fresh when one day a placard appeared on the gate, announcing that the house, the chalet, and dependences were to be let or sold immediately.

The seasons succeeded each other, and still the placard swung in the wind. The sun and the rain wrinkled it and turned it yellow.

Then in the autumn days the silence of desolation fell on the hills of Meudon. Then, with heavy tread, musket on shoulder, and leather helmet on head, the German soldiers entered the abandoned chalet and took up their quarters there. They made fires in the furnace with the polished planks of the *parquets*. The roof was crushed by a shell. The great winter had come. France was invaded —Paris besieged. In this crumbling away of a people, the fortune of Fellaire disappeared for ever.

The cessation of all municipal work after the resignation of the Prefect of the Seine, under the ministry of Chevandier de Valdrôme, had already shaken the office in the Rue Neuve des Petits Champs to its foundations. Luck had forsaken Fellaire, and he let himself go with the stream. He gave up dyeing his whiskers, and wore dusty frock-coats and tortoiseshell-mounted spectacles. He would stake in gambling dens the stray louis he still picked up here and there. Now that his daughter

no longer kept his house, he received visits from
ladies with yellow hair and painted faces, who sang
on the stairs. He was seen one day at the Folies-
Bergères with a woman on each arm. During
the siege of Paris he became serious again, and
started an insurance company, "The Phœnix of
the National Guard." But no one paid any
attention to it.

.   .   .   .   .   .

Hélène was married. She had been travelling for
four years; the easy, careless life suited her. Tall,
beautiful, dressed with a severe magnificence, she
was much admired in hotels and casinos, where
her indifference lent her an aristocratic air. She
endeavoured to care for her husband. But though
he was the most honourable and upright of men, he
was terribly tiresome. He saw, heard, said and
accomplished everything with equal gravity. Nothing was great or small in his eyes; everything
was worthy of being taken into consideration.
He would give his wife diamond ornaments, and
then tease her childishly for ten hours about a
sum of three francs which she could not account
for. He made handsome presents in a narrow
way, even his prodigalities wore an avaricious
look. He interfered in all the extravagances of his
young bride—not to check them, but to register
them. He allowed her to spend lavishly, but on

condition that she fulfilled every formality.   A
third of his life was spent in disputing about
ha'pennies with hotel waiters.   He was obstinately
determined not to be robbed of a sou; and would
willingly have ruined himself to foil the would-be
robber.   He calculated everything—distances to
within a yard, longitudes and latitudes, heights, the
rise and fall of the barometer, the number of
degrees marked on the thermometer, the direction
of the wind, the position of the clouds.   At Naples
he surveyed Virgil's tomb like a land surveyor.
He had a mania for neatness, and could not bear to
see a newspaper open on a sofa.   He exasperated
Hélène by picking up and returning to her twenty
times a day the book or the embroidery which she
had laid down.   It made her think regretfully of
her father, who would forget that he had put the
stumps of his cigars on the damask arm-chairs.
But all this was as nothing.

Hélène's great trouble was being forced to live
with a man so absolutely devoid of imagination.
The faculty was so foreign to Mr. Haviland that
he was incapable of describing a sentiment or giving
any interest to a thought.   Since their marriage he
had never opened his mouth, except to enunciate
some direct, precise, and timely fact.   No doubt
he was very much in love, and very proud of his
wife; but his love was like a fine rain: one of those

kinds of rain which one neither sees nor hears—
unceasing, penetrating, chilling.

Mr. Haviland's personal attendant was a French-
man named Groult. He came from Avranches, and
had been many years in his service. They had
travelled twice round the world together and were
inseparable.

Groult was not handsome. He had stiff, flaming-
red hair, shifty green eyes, and walked with a limp;
but he was of an exemplary cleanliness, and fulfilled his functions with perfect exactitude. He
was married; his wife was also in Mr. Haviland's
service. She remained in Paris and looked after
the house he had built recently on the Boulevard
Latour-Maubourg.

Mr. Haviland was much interested in chemistry,
and Groult helped him in the laboratory. He had
a mania for drenching himself with medicine daily,
and Groult looked after his travelling pharmacy.
Besides manipulating drugs with much ability, he
was adroit in many ways, and was even a good
locksmith when occasion required. His horrible
bony hands, with their enormous thumbs, could
execute the most delicate tasks; but though endowed with an extraordinary aptitude for mechanical
arts, he could never learn to write in the least degree
legibly. He had composed an alphabet for himself
which he alone could understand, and it was im-

possible to make out a letter or a figure of his
accounts, which he scribbled on scraps of paper.
The cooks and housemaids detested him because of
his scrawls, his horrible hands, his lameness, the
spots the chemicals left on his skin, and the smell of
drugs with which he was impregnated; they nick-
named him "Clochon," and feared him like the
devil; they considered him capable of any crime,
but could find nothing to reproach him with.
Groult was impeccable.

He inspired Hélène with an instinctive repug-
nance, and at first she tried to have him dismissed,
but soon saw that he was indispensable to her
husband, and resigned herself to the sight of him
limping perpetually between her husband and herself. He did not appear to bear her any malice,
and never comported himself towards her otherwise
than as a perfect servant.

Madame's wish to be rid of him had not
frightened him very much. He possessed the
confidence of his master, who he knew would not
separate from him lightly. There was a tie between Haviland and his servant Groult. For
twenty years they had been searching together for
Samuel Ewart.

.　　　.　　　.　　　.　　　.　　　.

Haviland was still a child when he heard for
the first time the story of the old cashier David

Ewart, and of his death on the scaffold in 1794.
The sublime obstinacy of this brave man, quietly
awaiting his doom while keeping the books his
masters had confided to him, appeared most praise-
worthy to the heir of the house of Haviland, whose
sense of fitness and tenacity of purpose just fitted
him to understand such practical devotion. He
showed nothing of what he felt at the moment;
but later on, when he had become master of his
actions and his fortune, he began to search actively
for some living descendant of the old cashier. He
learnt that Andrew Ewart, great-grandson of David,
was alive and settled as a merchant in Calcutta.
Andrew had married an Anglo-Indian, and had gone
into partnership with a Brahmin; their business was
carried on under the name of Andrew Ewart,
Liçaliçali & Company. Haviland, accompanied
by Groult, took the steamer to Calcutta, with the
intention of finding Andrew and saying to him:
"Your great-grandfather died in the service of
mine, like a perfect gentleman. Allow me to
shake you by the hand. Can I be of use to you
in any way?"

When he arrived in Calcutta in 1849, he learnt
that the firm of Andrew Ewart, Liçaliçali & Company had been dissolved by the decease of Andrew,
who had died of cholera in June 1848, leaving a
widow and a four-year-old son named Samuel;

but Haviland could find no further trace of them.
Mrs. Andrew, having been left unprovided for,
had quitted Calcutta with her little child. Having
learnt that Liçaliçali had settled in the Isle of
Bourbon he went there, and found the Brahmin
giving English lessons to the children of the
governor of the colony. Liçaliçali told Haviland
that Ewart's widow and son were living with her
brother—a Mr. Johnson, a former officer in Her
Majesty's service; beyond this he could hear
nothing.

Every week an advertisement appeared in the
Times, inviting Samuel Ewart (who at the time of
Hélène's marriage must have been about twenty-
seven years old) to present himself, or make known
his place of residence to Martin Haviland, Esq.,
Paris ; but Samuel Ewart gave no sign of life.

For twenty-five years Haviland pursued his researches, with no more apparent ardour or fatigue
than when he entered on them. It was his task,
and he took it up every morning as a carpenter
takes up his plane. Groult held the threads of
the affair in his hands, and disentangled them
skilfully. He was particularly useful when it came
to showing the door to some false Samuel Ewart ;
for many adventurers presented themselves to
Haviland, as being the son and heir of the late
Andrew.

Haviland's health became very bad in the autumn of the year 1871 ; he suffered from giddiness and insomnia. One day (it was at the beginning of the winter ; they were living at Nice in the Villa des Oliviers) Hélène, who was reading a novel in the drawing-room, gave a cry of horror as her husband came in.

"Your eyes!" she said. "Look at your eyes in the glass!"

Haviland's blue eyes had turned black. His lips were trembling, and he seemed to be wandering in his mind as he murmured :

"Sam—Sam Ewart; he will come."

CHAPTER IV

THEY returned to Paris for the rest of the winter. The courtyard of the hotel was full of trunks, cases, and packages; their size and number filled Madame Groult with despair as she moved about among them. She wore a bed-jacket of flowered calico, and her body seemed as limp as the stuff which covered it. Madame Groult, flabby and agitated, resembled a bundle of rags moved by some invisible force.

Her face was perpetually bathed in a sort of steam, and she continually wiped it with her cottony forearm. She arranged the bonnet-boxes according to the directions of the lady's-maid; but naturally timid, the orders and counter-orders she received only made her lose her head, while the frizzy-haired maid, her cap-strings flung coquettishly back, made eyes at the grooms.

Hélène threw her travelling mantle on an arm-chair, and Mr. Haviland promptly took it up and folded it neatly. She turned impatiently to the window, and began to beat " The Turkish Patrol "

on the glass. The dome of Les Invalides glimmered
faintly under the foggy sky. All around was dull
and grey, and she went sulkily away to her own
room.

Groult announced Monsieur Fellaire de Sisac.
The business man had come in haste to salute his
son-in-law and embrace his daughter. He was buttoned up to the throat. His cracked and broken top-
hat was beyond being treated with an iron, so water
had been tried. It had been literally soaked, to make
the rebellious nap lie down and to give it a little shine.
The heels of Monsieur Fellaire's boots were worn
down to such an extent that he was forced to walk
like a duck in order to maintain his equilibrium.

Haviland did not offer him his hand.

Fellaire tried every means to warm up "his dear
islander"—"his most highly-respected son-in-law."
His metallic voice sounded like the striking of flint
and steel, but he could get no spark out of Haviland. He said to himself that, after all, this devil
of a man was naturally taciturn, and persisted obstinately in his efforts to electrify him. Seeing that
no inquiry was made as to the state of his affairs,
he said at last :

" By-the-bye, I won't conceal from you the fact
that I have been through some very rough times lately.
I have been through what one might call a crisis."

He could not very well conceal difficulties of

this kind from Haviland, whom he had pursued with demands for money for the last four years. During the siege he had applied for a draft on a Paris banker by balloon, by carrier-pigeon, by advertisements in the *Daily Telegraph*. Haviland had satisfied the first demand, the others he had not even replied to.

So Fellaire presented himself at Mr. Charles Simpson's bank, Rue de la Victoire, and by using the beloved and respected name of his son-in-law, borrowed a considerable sum. This artifice seemed to Haviland intolerably unworthy.

Fellaire therefore did not attempt to hide his troubles, but he said he had surmounted them, and had now a magnificent affair in hand. He assumed an attitude suited to the importance of the subject, stuck his arms akimbo, and drew a long breath.

"It is a matter," he said, fixing a Napoleonic look on the ceiling, "the essentially beneficent aspect of which will not escape you. It is a question of opening a working-men's bank on an entirely new basis. At an epoch when the over-rapid advance of the labouring classes has become embarrassing to the political economist, and presents, if I may say so, a permanent menace to society, the need becomes self-apparent for some institution which will inspire the proletariat with the sentiment of thrift. Freed now from the obstacles which the preceding govern-

ment would certainly have put in the way of the
foundation of an establishment of this nature, the
moment has come in which to act——"

Just then a ray of sunlight—the only one in the
salon, perhaps in the whole house—fell treacherously
on Fellaire's wretched hat, and showed it up in all
its misery. He paused for a moment, then continued energetically :

" And to act quickly."

He asked Haviland if he would like to hear the
statutes of the proposed "working-men's bank."

Haviland answered, " No ! "

Fellaire insisted that he should at least let him
give a general idea of the way in which the bank was
to be organised. He looked to his son-in-law for
some valuable advice. And why not speak frankly ?
The business was worthy the attention of capitalists
of the first rank, and he was anxious that Haviland
should benefit by the advantages reserved for the
original shareholders.

When he had finished speaking, Haviland rang
the bell, the man-servant limped in.

" Groult," he said, " take away that cigar."

It was the stump of a much chewed penny cigar,
which Fellaire on entering had deposited on the
edge of a console table.

Haviland then looked Fellaire squarely in the
face and said :

" I will not give you any advice, because you would not listen to it. I will not give you any money, because you would not pay me back. You are not a gentleman—no ! I beg you never to enter my house again. You can see Madame Haviland when and where you please."

And he left the room.

Fellaire, though upset and staggered by this blow, feeling that everything had come to an end, yet had the courage to kiss his daughter gaily and keep up a few moments' chat about trifles. She received him with the tenderness of a child. In his easy-going nature there was something which corresponded with her laziness, and after all he was her father. With one glance of her woman's eye she had noted the ragged edges of his linen, the worn collar of his coat, the shabby hat—all the sordid details of his costume. She guessed the truth. But seeing her suspicious, he smiled—poor man, he spoke of the vast enterprises which were absorbing him. He accused himself of becoming negligent of his appearance as he grew older. He asked if she were happy, and told her to love her husband. Then, having embraced her effusively, he went downstairs with a heavy step—his back bent, his eyes dull, his chin dropped, his head hanging under his everlasting hat ; he had aged by at least ten years.

Hélène saw that her husband and father had

disagreed, and, although she guessed the cause of the rupture, she took part against Haviland. From that moment husband and wife began to bicker and exchange bitter allusions ; they would quarrel without any apparent motive, so that explanations were out of the question.

As she had sudden emotional outbursts, she transferred her wasted affections abruptly to her husband's nephew, George Haviland—a smart, good-looking, blonde boy, with a loving but sulky nature. He was born at Avranches, and had been brought up in the Catholic religion, in the midst of the little English colony there. He was an orphan, and his uncle, who was also his guardian, had placed him as a day-scholar at the Collège Stanislas. Hélène spoilt him with the best intentions in the world. She would arrange his hair herself twenty times a day, to see which fashion suited him best. She would make him leave his studies in the evening to accompany her to a concert or to the theatre.

But her days were empty, and she often wept from sheer ennui. She would have liked to live in a garret alone with her father, and would run off in secret to visit him. He was living, for the time being, rent free—" drying the plaster " on the fourth storey of a new house in the Rue de Rome. These expeditions, on which she went trembling, and with her veil down, as though to a rendezvous, amused

her immensely. Her father's rooms looked like a
bachelor's lodgings; there were pipes among the
papers on the table, the faded sofa was inviting and
soft in spite of its broken springs. After she had
kissed him on his big heavy cheeks, she would
rummage in every corner. If she discovered some
feminine object, such as a parasol or a veil, she
would pass over it, and with tight lips but laughing eyes pretend not to notice it. Her father
watched her, in mute admiration and love. When
she had turned over the papers, eaten the cakes,
had something to drink, laughed, and pulled his
whiskers, she would heave a deep sigh and depart;
and he, settling his disarranged smoking-cap, would
go with her to the landing and whisper at parting,
"Love your husband, my dear; love him with all
your heart."

As a matter of fact, she detested her husband.
Leaning back in the cab, she would imagine him
sitting in front of her, back to back with the
cabman, with his lifeless eyes, and his cheeks like
underdone beef, and would make a little grimace
expressive of disgust.

Was there in the bottom of her soul, in the region
of bygone days, the image of a countenance, half
effaced by time, but still loveable, dear, the face of
one who has departed never to return? Among the
longings of this wearied woman were there perhaps

some which groping out towards one being went a far far journey yet never reached their goal?

One day, when she had let a piece of embroidery, begun long since, fall to her knees as though it were too heavy a burden, she was noting with that fixed intentness associated with ennui the imperceptible irregularities of the glass in the window panes which, looked at sideways, seemed to waver into architectural outlines. Presently her maid brought her a visiting card from someone who had called and wished to see her.

She glanced at the card, sprang up, adjusted her curls, settled the pleats of her skirt, and went down to the drawing-room, transformed and animated, with a swan-like grace in the poise of her head, and a queenly sweep of her trailing robes.

CHAPTER V

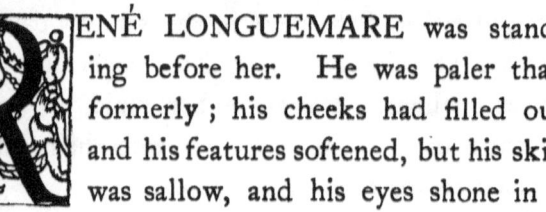ENÉ LONGUEMARE was standing before her. He was paler than formerly; his cheeks had filled out and his features softened, but his skin was sallow, and his eyes shone in a dark circle ploughed by fever contracted in the rice fields; he had still his old frank look, his wide affectionate smile, and his outspoken manner.

"You see," she said to him, "the world is small, and one comes back from the furthermost parts of it. I am not surprised to see you, but I am very, very pleased."

They were ill at ease at first. Each one had lived a long span of life, of the details of which the other knew nothing. They sought about for common ground. She was the first to risk a cordial phrase, perhaps because she felt it her duty as mistress of the house, perhaps because she was tempted by some secret sentiment.

"I have often thought of you," she said. Then René plunged boldly into their mutual recollections. He spoke of the cups of tea at the house in the

Rue Neuve des Petits Champs, of their walks at
Meudon, of her pink and white muslin frocks which
the brambles tore, of Monsieur Fellaire's fine waistcoats, which they would make a rallying point on
their excursions through the woods, as though it
were the white plume of the Béarnais; and of all
the nonsense they talked. She asked him if he
still kept frogs in his pockets, and at the end of
a quarter of an hour it seemed as though they
had never been separated. When he began to tell
her quietly of his travels, and of the monotonous
fatigue of his service on an unhealthy station,
she opened her beautiful humid eyes wide as she
listened. Then she asked what he intended to
do. He was tired, he said, of military service.
He should send in his resignation, and settle down
as a country doctor and village bone-setter : if some
very innocent young girl had a fancy for raising
poultry under his protection, he would marry her.

"Ah!" she said quickly, "you want to get
married ? "

But she knew from his answers that he was not
serious; he had some great void in his heart, some
sorrow, perhaps some souvenir.

George came back from school and burst in
upon them with his lesson-books, then settled himself like a spoiled child to enjoy the distraction that
this gentleman offered him. Hélène did not send

him away, but told him to keep quiet and do his
work. The doctor was relating an episode of his
voyage, and the boy, noisily turning over the leaves
of his dictionary, was biting his penholder and turning his head as he listened to a story of sea-spiders
eaten alive by one of the sailors on the deck of the
ship, when the maid came in to say that Mr.
Haviland was ill, and begged Madame to go to him
at once.

Mr. Haviland's bedroom was very large, and
filled with strange objects, all arranged in precise
order. There was a cabinet full of sealed and
labelled bottles. He had collected half a bottle
of water from all the rivers he had crossed, and
one could read on the labels — Tagus, Jordan,
Simois, Eurotas, Tiber, Ohio. Another cabinet contained specimens of the marbles of the world.
There was also a cupboard dedicated to historical
souvenirs, and containing stones from Tasso's
prison, Shakespeare's birthplace, Joan of Arc's
hut, the tomb of Héloïse, leaves from the weeping
willow of Saint Helena, a piece of poetry written
by Lacenaire in the Conciergerie, a travelling-clock
stolen from the Tuileries in 1848, a comb which had
belonged to Mademoiselle Rachel; and in a glass
tube, a hair from the head of Joseph Smith the
Mormon prophet, besides other relics too numerous
to be specified. Several large tables, made of pine

wood, such as architects use for drawing-tables, were covered with phials, and the whole place exhaled a very pronounced pharmaceutical odour.

Haviland was lying on a sofa near his iron bedstead, a travelling rug over his legs. He was livid, save for the red patches on his cheeks. His eyes, unnaturally sombre, seemed to be starting from their orbits. He took hold of his wife's hands with the eager tenderness of a person who feels that everything is slipping away from him. He told her that he loved her, and was grateful to her; that he felt very ill, but hoped to recover, as he was well taken care of, and followed a treatment of his own which Groult knew how to apply. Then an attack of giddiness cut short his speech.

By-and-by he went on :

"I ought to warn you, Hélène, that I have wandering moments. They are a feature of my disease. You must take no notice of anything I may do at such times. Fortunately my affairs are in order. My will is with my notary."

He then told her that he had left her the income accruing from his fortune for her life, but that the capital, as was only right, was to go to George Haviland. He had also made a disposition in favour of his servant Groult, and had told him about it. He pressed his wife's hand, and fixing on her the strange and dolorous look he sometimes wore, begged her to listen carefully to what he was about to say.

"Out of respect for my memory if I die, my dear Hélène, look for Samuel Ewart, and execute my last wishes in his favour. In the name of our Lord and Saviour, Jesus Christ, who will come again to raise the dead, I conjure you to neglect nothing which may ensure that the last descendant of David Ewart shall receive the money I have bequeathed him. I know he is alive, for sometimes of nights I see him. I should recognise him were he to come, and he will come."

Suddenly the sick man fixed his eyes on a dark curtain which hung in heavy folds before a door, stretched out his trembling arm, and cried :

"There! there! before that door! There he is, there's Sam Ewart. You can see the mark he bears on his neck, under his sailor's shirt; it is a red mark because of his great-grandfather, old David —Sam! Sam! Oh my God!"

He fell back on the sofa breathing heavily. Hélène, who felt helpless and lost among the many medicine bottles, rang for Groult, who pushed her aside, rudely enough, and took possession of the invalid.

That night she could not sleep. As she lay

watching the moonlight, she saw her husband, wrapped in a plaid, come down through his bedroom window, and walk straight to a well by the stables.

As she watched him breathlessly, her face pressed against the glass, she was conscious of a sharp pain at the roots of her hair, but could neither move nor cry out. Then she saw Groult come, half-dressed, from the outbuilding where he slept, and follow his master on tiptoe. She saw the latter peering down into the depths of the well. After some time he raised his head, and stretched his hand out as though to feel from which quarter the wind was blowing, after which he went back through the window to his room. She saw Groult shrug his shoulders and slouch off to his outbuilding, with a contemptuous gesture.

Madam Groult had appeared for a moment in her everlasting bed-jacket and an enormous frilled night-cap at the door of the lodge. When the door had closed upon them both Hélène thought she heard Groult ill-treating her.

Haviland had become a somnambulist.

The next day she found him up and dressed, peacefully and silently occupied in labelling numerous little stones which he had taken from famous monuments. He was writing on gummed paper the words "Coliseum," "Catacombs," "Tomb of Cecilia

Metella." His eyes which had recovered their normal colour, a dull blue, were quite expressionless.

But she did not feel reassured. She wanted to remain by him, and determined to sit by him herself and send for doctors, although he had strictly forbidden her to do so.

Groult came into the room with a bottle and a glass, from which he poured some syrup and handed it to his master, looking fixedly at Hélène the while. He watched her with a cynical familiarity, an audacious effrontery, that made her blush. A little while after drinking the syrup, Haviland was seized with giddiness and stupor. His pupils once more became extraordinarily dilated.

From this day, Hélène was tormented with a vague uneasiness. One evening, about five o'clock, she noticed the tracks of nailed shoes on the carpet of the room. The steps went in an oblique line right across the room from the outer door to that of the dressing-room. The tracks were extremely faint, and only visible because the rays of the sun were at that moment falling on the carpet, showing up the slight signs of pressure and the specks of white dust on the rich, soft Smyrna tissue. She was startled and called her maid, and they inspected the dressing-room minutely, but everything was in order For some time she tried to explain to herself the meaning of these footsteps, but as she could find no solution to the problem, she tired of troubling herself, and fell back into her accustomed indifference.

When René Longuemare returned, Hélène, who was expecting him, had dressed her hair in the way in which she knew he liked it best. She could not hide her unhappiness from him, and weakly told him all the misery of her life, and how wretchedly her marriage had turned out. She knew that she loved him. She would have liked to be gathered to his broad, warm chest, to weep there, and forget everything. René remained very calm by the side of her. The more she confided in him, the more he felt that he must not abuse her confidence. He loved her respectfully ; she represented the poetry of his bachelor's existence, where prose was not wanting. He had taken up his old habits in Paris, and every night he went to some little theatre, and to supper afterwards. There was a spacious and lofty place in his soul for an ideal creature, and in this place he had put Hélène. On her side, though tired and weak, abased in her own eyes by a loveless marriage, but reserved according to the habits of her class and circumspect from preference, she kept well under when in René's company whatever tendencies she might feel towards the too alluring or the too encouraging. So far exempt from all fault,

E

it seemed to her quite impossible to contemplate
committing one.

When she spoke to him of her husband's illness,
René shook his head. It was probable that Mr.
Haviland was treating himself wrongly. According
to the symptoms described to him, the army doctor's
diagnosis was that it was not a case of a natural
disease following its usual course; he was inclined
to attribute it rather to the intermittent action of
some injurious agent, some poison. The dilatation
of the pupil seemed to him to be unquestionably
due to an immoderate use of belladonna or atropine.
To fight against his rheumatism, Haviland had
evidently made use of chloro-hydrated sulphate of
atropine, and now according to appearances was
making a most disastrous abuse of this drug.

Hélène resolved to act on René's urgent advice
to call in a doctor, also to nurse the sick man
herself.

The following day she found him in an attic
which he used as a workshop. He was planing
a board with the greatest care, for he was a
carpenter as well as a chemist. Seeing him so
calm and rested, she thought she must have been
dreaming. He talked about the cook, who was
a thief, and whom he had sent away; it was
Groult who had discovered his peculations. Every
now and then he would lay his plane down on

the bench and delicately remove a shaving caught
in the guipure of his wife's dressing-gown. His
eyes were clear and normal, and he had never
shown such a lack of imagination.

She thought of René, so lively, so intelligent,
his mind as full of interesting things as a well
written book, his soul bursting with youth and
strength; and her heart swelled with hate when
she looked at the old man bent over his plane.
Groult came at the usual time to bring his master
his syrup. When he saw Hélène in the attic, where
she had never before put her foot, he rolled his
eyes at her like a furious cat.

Then, as on a previous occasion, while Haviland
was drinking his syrup, he looked at her impudently,
and growled something between his twisted lips.
He was so ugly and so cynical that there and then
in a flash she understood clearly and certainly without any question what it was he was doing.

She stretched out her hand, as though to snatch
the glass from the old man's lips. Groult whispered
in her ear, in an ill-mannered and menacing tone:

" Don't be childish."

She stood still, incapable of moving, white to
the lips. Haviland finished the syrup and wiped
his mouth.

The miserable woman rushed down the stairs,
overcome, giddy, feeling as though at each step

she would fall through the ground, frightened at her own immeasurable cowardice.

She did not dare to reappear before her husband : she heard that evening from her maid that he had been violently delirious, but that then he was resting. She had imagined him to be dead, and heaved a sigh of relief. She said to herself, "He lives; there is still time to speak, to act. I will not be the accomplice of a . . ."

Her nerves had been stretched beyond endurance, and she sank down exhausted and heavy with sleep. She thought of René, and her imagination pictured him clothed with all the visionary charm and magic of an absent loved one; her thoughts grew confused and painful. Her head was burning, yet she shivered and her teeth chattered. She experienced a sensation akin to joy, as she slipped into bed; then she lost all grasp on reality. She saw terrible figures passing so quickly she had not time to recognise them. Where was she? And what did this crowd of strangers, dressed in all sorts of theatrical costumes, want with her? Something hot, which she kept pushing from her with horror, weighed on her chest and stifled her. It was a red cat whose eyes kept changing colour. She stuck out her elbows and bent her knees.

A nun came and straightened her bedclothes, but what was she doing there? There were two

or three others, who prevented her from going out;
yet she had something most important to do, something which could not be put off for one moment,
though she was no longer sure what it was.

"Oh, my head! my poor head!" she cried.
She was suffering so in her brain that she looked
about for a wall, an iron wall, against which to
strike her skull, and thus obtain relief. Oh! quick!
If she could only make a good wide crack in it so
as to let out the water which was boiling inside.
An unfamiliar voice said, "Yes, more ice"; but
she saw no ice. She was lost on a shore of burning
sand, on the edge of a sea of molten lead. She
called out, "René! René! take me to the woods
at Meudon! Have you forgotten the time when
you used to gather hawthorn there for me?"

She fell asleep. When she awoke she was quite
childish, and recited in the monotonous tone of a
schoolgirl bits of the Catechism and scraps of fables.

"I can't learn my lessons," she murmured.
"Madame, my head aches; let me go home. I
want to see Papa."

One day she found herself sitting up in bed,
very weak but very hungry. She learnt from the
nun who was nursing her that she had been very ill
for three weeks, but was now out of danger. She
made a great effort to collect her thoughts, and
asked:

"And my husband?"

The nun told her not to worry; he was well. Hélène breathed again.

During her convalescence she had several lapses of memory, and suffered from the great mental fatigue which ordinarily follows brain fever. There was only one clearly-defined feeling in her mind—terror at the thought of seeing her husband again. When she was told that Mr. Haviland, who was now convalescent himself, was coming to visit her in her room, she had a violent attack of palpitation of the heart. He looked at her affectionately, told her how much he loved her, and for the first time she saw a smile on his' grave face. The smile came from within, so profound and so true that she could not but be moved and touched by it. She began to cry, and, turning to the old man, like a loving child put her arms round his neck; but he had already regained his usual stiffness.

By dint of a great effort she recalled across the vapours of her mind the memory of the two potions she had seen Groult pour out. She took her husband's hands in her own and said to him supplicatingly:

"If you love me, if you wish to save us both from a horrible death, send away, I conjure you, your valet; send him away to-day, at once. What

he has done is horrible—horrible. I cannot speak
of it. Send him away; send him away."

Mr. Haviland remembered that Hélène had
always shown an aversion for the valet, and, seeing her so feeble, shaken by convulsive sobs and
half fainting, he decided that though she was speaking unreasonably it was necessary for him to sacrifice
his servant. He called him down from the laboratory and said to him:

"Groult, we must separate. I am quite satisfied
with you, and I should have liked to keep you with
me until my death—yes. But your presence in this
house has become impossible, for reasons which I
need not explain to you—no. I shall not change in
any way the dispositions I have made in your favour.
I tell you so, and you may believe me. You will
leave the house on Friday. I will look after you
until you get another place. I should like your
wife to remain in my service, and I wish to continue
in direct communication with you on all matters
which concern Samuel Ewart. I have nothing more
to say."

Groult did not answer; he simply bent his head
and left the room.

CHAPTER VI

T was on a Friday that Groult was given notice to leave. On Saturday Haviland felt better than he had done for several months. He drove in the Bois de Boulogne with Hélène, whose health was now almost re-established.

The slight shaking of the carriage and the fresh air agreeably fatigued the two convalescents. Hélène was in the indifferent state born of lassitude. She accepted for the nonce with all her deadened heart the insipid husband and the monotonous fate which had fallen to her lot. Weakness brings with it such consolations. From sheer sick egoism she grew affectionate to the man seated by her side in the barouche, his knees under the fur rug which warmed her own. She glanced coldly at the trees, the lamp-posts, the foot-passengers whom the carriage left behind, at the houses in the Champs Élysées, with their coachmakers' showrooms, at the sanded alleys, where bowlegged grooms were leading horses up and down by the bridle in the shade; then at the Arc de Triomphe dominating the open space around it with heavy emphasis; then, to the left, at the avenue leading to the Bois, bordered on each side by a band of English gardens; she could see, to the right, horsemen galloping on the gravelled paths: all was bathed in the spring sunlight. The watering-pipes had already made their appearance, and men were dragging the long tubes on their little castors about the roads and sprinkling the legs of the half-frightened horses. Sometimes the wind and the shadow of a rapidly driven victoria passed over her face. A pale girl with red hair and painted lips, with her elbows well in as she held the reins, would drive quickly by, a groom with folded arms seated behind her. When the fresh air of the Bois was reached they drove more slowly; carriages gay with tiger skins, with bright spring toilets and happy faces followed one behind the other at a foot-pace. Salutations were exchanged between one carriage and another, smiling cavaliers bent down to talk to women lying back on the soft cushions beneath the shade of the lowered hoods. A workman's wedding-party went by on foot, in couples, in the opposite direction.

The stiffly-correct attitude of Haviland was not displeasing to Hélène; she liked his impassibility and his good style. The silence of the man, the calm expression of his face, the simplicity of his ideas pleased her now as so many delicate attentions bestowed on a convalescent. He was dearer to her now she felt she had saved his life. She was afraid of thinking too deeply, and enjoyed the delights of a restricted fatigue and a daily increasing strength. She cosetted herself with the luxuriousness of a chilly cat.

They got out at the Cascade, and drank a glass of milk at the Café.

The tables on each side of them were occupied by whispering old men and the rustle of dresses intermingled with the faint murmur of chattering women. In front of her three young fellows were talking at the top of their voices. She did not know the two facing her, but the one whose back was turned to her and who was almost wholly hidden by one of the waiters she recognised by the outline of his shoulders.

She felt a painful inward spasm, and something in her throat seemed to stifle her, the blood rushed hotly to her cheeks, an indescribable anguish which was at the same time a rapture of overpowering delight took possession of her.

Longuemare, the cause of all this trouble, was far from thinking she was so near him, and went on with the conversation so noisily begun, exaggerating outrageously, as was his habit, his views on the subject under discussion.

"The only practitioner whom I admire," he said

to his comrades (who seemed, like himself, to have been lunching well), "the only one, is Pinel. He never gave any medicine to his patients for fear of checking the normal course of their disease. Satisfied if he could describe and classify a lesion, he prudently abstained from attempting to heal it. Before the magnificent progress of an open wound he remained attentive, respectful, motionless. What a doctor Pinel was!"

René's voice was drowned in a burst of laughter; interruptions spouted forth and the three friends all began to talk at once. Hélène's throat grew dry, there was a buzzing in her head, her sight failed her, and perspiration broke out on her brow. Her husband, seeing her so pale, asked if she was tired, if she wished to return home. She looked at him, and he appeared odious to her. His face was covered with a network of little violet veins, and his cheeks were white and scaly, his eyes were dim and vacant: she almost regretted his recovery now.

When they rose up to go, Longuemare saw her; the look which he exchanged with Hélène seemed to draw them closely together.

The next day the old man could not leave his bed; all the symptoms of his intermittent malady had returned, and in a few days they became alarming. On Friday morning Hélène sent for a

doctor. Her husband's appearance was alarming;
his eyes were bloodshot and half out of their
sockets ; he was raving in delirium.

Dr. Hersent, who came while the attack was at
its worst, gave him an antispasmodic and sedative
medicine, which produced no visible effect. He
declared that the case was very grave, that there
was probably a profound lesion in the nerve centres,
and, fearing that a serious termination might swiftly
succeed his visit, insisted on holding a consultation
that very evening. Just at this time Groult, having
got his wife to attend to his packing, had taken
a cab and was leaving the house in accordance with
the orders he had received.

Hélène remained with the sick man. Crushed by
a nameless terror, she dared not look at him ; then,
suddenly seized with horrible curiosity, she stared
at him with all her eyes ; she must see—see what
was passing, even if it killed her. The unhappy
Haviland was struggling with two men-servants,
who by great efforts kept him between the bedclothes. He was calling for his wife and for
Samuel Ewart. Every note in his voice was
altered ; it sounded like the voice of another
man and by so much the more appalling. He
would whisper Hélène's name plaintively, and the
next moment would break into shrill yells and
sinister laughter. The contrast was so sudden it

was impossible to understand how even a madman could change so rapidly from sad tenderness to furious irony. Horrible enough as the scene was in reality, Hélène's sick imagination increased it tenfold. She felt as if red hot wires were running from her head to her heels; a burning garment wrapped her round behind and before.

She listened attentively to what her husband was saying, but was the more distressed that she could not discover the vaguest meaning in his wanderings. If at that moment he had pointed his finger at her, denounced her openly and cursed her, it would have been a positive relief.

At ten o'clock in the evening the doctors, Hersent, Guérard, and Baldec, were gathered round the patient, who, in their presence, was seized with a trembling in every limb; then he sank back and appeared to be sleeping. A new torment, the worst of all, began for Hélène. All the old feelings of friendship and respect for the man who had so loyally loved her returned. She could not help weeping, yet her tears disgusted her; they were hypocritical tears, for was she not to blame?

Haviland's breathing was so rapid and so painful that all who heard it, with the exception of the doctors, felt oppressed. His bony hands were spread on the counterpane and scratched and plucked clumsily at it. Dr. Hersent took his left wrist;

the pulse was weaker, his extremities were growing
cold. His nose was pinched, his eyes sunk in. He
rolled them round as though to see and recognise
things for one last time, then he dropped his head
back on the pillow and sighed three times. A
gesture from the doctor announced that all was
over; he was at rest.

When Hélène, who had been standing stiffly upright throughout his death agony, heard that he was
dead, she felt a delicious sensation; it was as though
the ground was opening beneath her and she was
slipping away into nothingness. How sweet to cease
from troubling, to cease *to be*: she fell fainting to
the ground.

As the doctors, Guérard and Baldec, were leaving
the house, they met a short gentleman, with big
whiskers and tortoiseshell-mounted spectacles, in
the hall. He took them by the hand and said with
a solemn accent:

"Gentlemen, your efforts have been in vain;
human skill, no matter how great it may be, has
its limits. The princes of science cannot control
Nature. I am one of those who respect courage
even in defeat. I declare to you that Fellaire de
Sisac will never forget the enlightened care you
have lavished on his honourable and sympathetic
son-in-law."

Then Monsieur Fellaire marched with a slow

grave step to the dining-room, where he ordered a light repast to be served to him.

Madame Groult, bathed in sweat and tears, was clucking mournfully in her lodge.

Dr. Hersent followed Hélène to her room, for he considered that her condition demanded some attention. When she saw this tall man all in black, whom she did not recognise, come in, she became delirious with fear. She stretched out her arms to him and shrieked:

"It was not I who did it! I swear to you it was not I!"

CHAPTER VII

ONSIEUR FELLAIRE showed immense activity after the death of his son-in-law. Attired in deep mourning he walked, with the nephew of the deceased, at the head of the funeral procession. The cortège went slowly down the outer boulevards to the Montparnasse Cemetery, where Haviland, who had adopted his wife's country, had bought a grave for himself and her. Fellaire's face was white and puffy from lack of sleep; he was not accustomed to rise so early in the morning. His reddened eyes and swollen eyelids behind his tortoiseshell spectacles gave an opportune expression of fatigue and melancholy to his face. Being stout, he naturally walked slowly and pompously. Aware of this advantage he made no effort to subdue or conceal his bulky importance. By a strange freak of fortune he was now able to wear a hat very different from that which he had deposited on the table in Haviland's drawing-room; the one he now carried was new and lustrous, with an immaculate lining. It lay on

his arm like a gun on its carriage and appeared to
be levelled at the hearse. His boots did not creak
as loudly as usual; they only emitted a sort of
discreet sigh at each step as though the funeral
genii were hidden in them. He stood motionless before the Gothic tomb, his eyes behind their
spectacles turned to heaven with a spiritual expression, while the workmen let the coffin down, spitting
on their hands as the cords ran through them,
and murmuring their " Oh's " and " Eh's " under
their breath. One understood by his attitude that
his thoughts had passed beyond the bronze portals
of the mausoleum and were floating on wings of
sublime philosophy in ethereal regions. He was
wandering thus in the domain of idealism, detached
from earthly existence, when a little fit of coughing
reminded him that he still lived and was tight in
the chest. Behind him and towering above him by
a head was a group of fair-haired, large-framed
Englishmen, erect and stiff in their well-cut clothes.
Two business men, *habitués* of the Brasserie de
Colmar and constant companions of Fellaire's at
billiards and dominoes, stood a little way off whispering together. The servants were huddled in the
pathway to the side of the tomb, and the sun,
shining strongly, showed up the footmen's whiskers
and the black ribbons in the maids' caps, revealed
sleeves that were too full and glimpses of black

trousers so much too long as to fall in great folds over the boots.

When the service was over, Fellaire received the complimentary condolences of those who had assisted at it with the air of a brave but heart-broken man.   He thanked those who had joined him in paying the last duties to the deceased.   He seemed to recognise the presence of each person with particular satisfaction, although he did not know one among them.   He shook their hands with an energy which was evidently meant to express, "Thank you—thank you.   I will have courage; I will bear up."   Only, when it was the turn of his old tavern companions, he barely accorded them the tips of his fingers, and frowningly repelled their expression of sympathy; he was afraid they would slap him on the shoulder and call him "Poor old chap."

He repeated his collective thanks many times, and finally addressed them to an assembly of persons who had been burying a magistrate, and who never understood what the singular gentleman in black wanted with them.

As it was impossible for him to distinguish between his son-in-law's friends and the rest of mankind, he would have gone on doing the honours of all the funerals throughout the day if they had happened to pass uninterruptedly before him.

From that time he never laid aside his mourning garments or his stoical and depressed mien. Every day he went to the Hôtel Haviland to luncheon and dinner. After dinner he would put his hand on George's head, and say with a sort of sob:

"This boy interests me."

At the Brasserie de Colmar, where he played billiards in the evening, he would often exclaim:

"It is not only a son-in-law that I have lost; it is a son—and a gentleman."

. . . . . .

Julia, Madame Haviland's maid, must have heard the strange cry her mistress gave on the appearance of the doctor in her room; for the next day there were mysterious whisperings at the grocer's and butcher's. The rumour that the Englishman of the Boulevard Latour-Maubourg had been poisoned, and that his wife was an accomplice of the crime, spread in a few days throughout the neighbourhood. Dr. Hersent, who lived in the Rue Saint-Dominic, was surprised upon the following Monday to hear his wife speak of the crime as a matter of general knowledge.

A long addiction to science and the practice of medicine had rendered Hersent careful in making researches, and he would not admit that there was, as a matter of fact, any reason to suspect Madame Haviland. He told his wife that it was against the etiquette of the profession to listen to such servants' gossip. At the same time, he was not quite easy in his mind; the disease to which Haviland had succumbed had not been sufficiently characterised in the burial certificate which he and the consulting physicians had signed, and he felt some qualms of self-reproach on the score of his negligence in this respect. He hoped that the affair would have no further consequences, and confidently reckoned that there would be none.

CHAPTER VIII

LONGUEMARE, whose morning visit at the hospital had been protracted longer than usual on account of an epidemic of typhoid fever, did not arrive at the Montparnesse Cemetery until the funeral of Mr. Haviland was over. All that he saw of the ceremony was the sombre and energetic profile of Fellaire being conveyed home from the cemetery in a carriage drawn by two black horses, placed at his disposal for the occasion by the undertakers.

Retracing his steps at this sight, he passed between the sculptured urns and hour-glasses over the entrance gates, when he was accosted by a sprightly little man, who, with a great deal of gaiety, hailed him as a ghost, a spectre and a phantom, and hummed in a fine grave voice the opening lines from the air in "Robert the Devil" —"Nuns who repose."

It was an old class-mate of his, Bouteiller, who, celebrated at school for his ineptitude in science and letters, had become a reporter on an important daily newspaper. He had just heard, or approximately heard, three speeches pronounced over the grave of a member of the Institute. Taking Longuemare by the arm, he said:

"My dear fellow, dine with me to-night at Bréval's."

During dinner Longuemare was profoundly agitated, but hid, as his habit was, his emotion under a joking exterior, and talked on many questions dealing with love and women in scientific language relieved by shocking puns; they drank champagne throughout the dinner. Bouteiller made a practice of doing so, and said this wine was a professional necessity for him. He was always extremely busy, and spent what should have been the best hours of his life on the railway. He inaugurated statues in every town in France, followed the President of the Republic into inundated departments, assisted at aristocratic weddings, listened to lectures on the phylloxera, saw and heard everything and remained the least curious of men. There was only one place in the world which interested him, and that was Chatou, where he had a cottage and a boat. He thought of nothing else, whereas he ought to have thought of the whole world. A factory could not burn down without him. Naturally, Longuemare was led to speak of Haviland and his singular habits, of his death, and

in a casual way, of poisoning by belladonna. At the
same time Bouteiller was describing his boat; they
understood each other perfectly. Towards ten
o'clock the journalist said:

"My dear fellow, I must run round to the office.
Wait for me at the Café de Suède; I have an appointment there."

At eleven they were both seated smoking at a
zinc table, in the noise and light of the boulevard.
Bouteiller was saying:

"You see you must have a rather short oar,
which you can get a good grip on, and above all,
thin at the end, so that it cuts the water like a
knife"; when a young lad in a blouse and cap
stopped in front of them and said:

"It is not to be to-night."

Bouteiller gave him a couple of francs and sent
him off. He seemed displeased.

"A special report which I had written up in
advance, and which is no good now."

Then by way of explanation he added:

"That young scamp knows how things are
done at La Roquette. He has just told me
that the man who committed the murder in the
Rue du Château-des-Rentiers will not be executed
to-night. By the way, you are a doctor; tell me
if you think one suffers after having one's head
cut off?"

"I can easily tell you that," said Longuemare, and he began a lengthy explanation.

"Life being a quantity, as Buffon says, it is susceptible to augmentation or diminution. The 'vital knot' Flourens talks of is rubbish. Now follow me carefully. If I say with Bichat that life is an assemblage of forces which resist death, I should add that these forces only resist for a longer or shorter period before final dissolution. Beheading produces a violent syncope, and abolishes sensibility in a measure which one may consider definite ; but at the same time muscular life goes on. You must not confound——"

Here Bouteiller in despair broke in :

"No, no; I'd rather tell you at once that your explanation is too long, and I don't understand a word of it. Science has always seemed to me terribly obscure. There are certain subjects, like the immortality of the soul, for instance, or the existence of God, which are so difficult. Fortunately God does not come into the news of the day —by-the-bye, what was the name of the Englishman you buried this morning ? I think I could make a good 'par.' out of what you told me, if I embroidered it a little. You were saying that . . .?"

CHAPTER IX

GROULT having roughly ordered his wife to pack his bag, left Paris for Avranches, where he said he had business to attend to. As a matter of fact, he had inherited a bit of land in a neighbouring village. He put up at an inn in the suburbs, called the Red Horse. Here he was to be seen drinking in the company of farmers and graziers, pouring the entire contents of a small spirit decanter into his coffee-cup in true Norman fashion. He was more gay and outspoken than usual, talked willingly to the folks about him, accepted their courtesies, and treated them to drinks.

On Wednesday he took the train to Granville, where he arrived at nightfall, in most frightful weather. A bad squall, the sailors said. It was raining, and a high wind was blowing the light aslant in the gas-lamps, and howling in the narrow alleys. He went towards the old part of the town, and turned up a steep, narrow, and winding street full of the smell of fish. His left foot as it fol-

lowed the right described the motion of a scythe
in a wheat field, and his whole body swung at every
step; still he went quickly on in the darkness,
grumbling and cursing as he splashed up the water
in the puddles.

By-and-by he came to a small, mean grocer's
shop, the blurred windows of which contained two
or three bottles of sweets; he went in without
hesitating. There was a wooden staircase in the
shop, with a bed covered in scarlet cotton, packed
under it. The sole entrance to the house was
through the shop, and its unflagged earthen floor
had crumbled in places and bore traces of heavily
nailed boots. No one was about, and Groult,
without losing time by waiting for the grocer,
mounted the stairs and knocked at a door on the
second storey, just where the banisters ended. A
little old man, holding a candle close under his chin,
examined the visitor through the half-opened door
before admitting him into a room encumbered
with packets of torn papers, dog-eared ledgers,
and burst and yawning portfolios, from which
protruded ends of ancient legal documents, all
heaped up and pressed solidly together. Piles of
dusty papers and parchments leant against the walls,
behind which one could hear the mice scurrying,
in spite of the noisy wind in the chimney and the
beating of the rain on the roof.

A mean and disordered bed, hung with ragged curtains, exposed its wretchedness and bareness in a shadowy corner. A thick layer of dust covered everything, making all objects uniformly grey; even the old man's face seemed to be spread with a coating of it. He was toothless, and his tongue moved and mumbled ceaselessly between his withered lips. His eyes were pale green, and their quick restlessness reminded one of the swift mice nibbling audibly behind the wainscoting.

"Well," said Groult, sitting down, "you wanted to speak to me; here I am. What's the news?"

The old man licked his gums slowly, and said in a drawling nasal voice:

"I am very pleased to see you, my good Monsieur Groult—perhaps there is some news, perhaps there isn't; it all depends upon how one looks at it."

He was twiddling his grey beard as he spoke, and seemed to be counting his words and the bristles in it at the same time.

Groult interrupted him with an impatient growl.

"Dear me!" said the other; "you are in a great hurry! As sure as my name is Tancrède Reuline, and yours is Desiré Groult, I am ready to tell you everything I know that may interest you. Daddy Reuline is known all along the coast, from Carolles point to the Bréhal fisheries. Big and little all come to me. I do business with gentle and

simple.   No later than yesterday I collected a debt
for Monsieur de Tancarville.   Ah! my dear sir, it
was what you might call a bad debt.   Monsieur
de Tancarville said to me in these very words,
'Reuline, I was going to light my pipe with it.'
And only last week the Baroness Dubosq-Marien-
ville——"

Groult interrupted by banging his fist down on
the table, and Reuline, after a moment in which
his lips moved without sound, went on in his
slow nasal drawl :

"Now we will come, if you please, to your business.   I am entirely at your disposition; we can't
possibly misunderstand each other.   I found for you
the birth certificate of a certain Mr. Samuel Ewart,
and sundry other papers, enabling one to identify
this person.   I gave you the papers from hand to
hand, as it were, without so much as asking what
use you were going to make of them.   I just did it
to be of service to you."

"What then?" asked Groult with a frown.

"Wait a bit—wait a bit," said the Norman.

He moistened his lips and continued :

"It's none of my business to inquire what interest
you had in Samuel Ewart's papers.   I am very
discreet, my good sir.   Discretion is one of the
leading virtues of my little trade.   But suppose
that Samuel Ewart is dead?"

"By God!" cried Groult, "if he is dead he won't come to life again"; and he burst out laughing.

"Wait a bit," said the old man (contemplating the pins carefully stuck in the sleeve of his coat) —"wait a bit. Suppose some person possesses a certified copy of his death certificate—the death certificate of Samuel Ewart who died in Jersey without descendants, and that the possessor of this paper can produce it at the right moment."

Groult spread out his enormous hands. He was exasperated at what he considered the treachery of his old accomplice, which seemed to make the other papers he had procured for him, at a great expense, useless.

"No tricks," he said roughly; "act square."

The Norman's eyes blinked uneasily, but he answered in a calm voice:

"Whatever I said was for your own good; but I see it makes you angry, so let's say no more about it and part good friends."

He got up, and took a lipless pitcher containing a bunch of forget-me-nots from a dilapidated walnut secretary.

"See," he said, putting the pitcher on the table, "they will last all the summer. Each time I go along the shore by Carteret, I gather a bunch in the ditch which runs by Monsieur de Laigle's grounds.

I wrap them up in my handkerchief. . . ." As he spoke, he passed his hand gently over the blue flowers and shook off the faded petals. " If one takes care to pull up the roots with the stalks, the plant will live in water as it would in the ground. Dear me! I have neither wife nor child, dog nor cat, and one must be fond of something—I'm fond of flowers."

Groult was not listening to him, he was biting his lips and gnawing at his nails. Suddenly he jumped up and shouted :

" You've got Samuel Ewart's death certificate. Give it me. I want it, and I will have it."

Reuline, with a furtive glance at the walnut secretary, put the pot of flowers carefully back in its place.

" Wait a bit," he said—" wait a bit. I have got the paper, and I haven't got it. Perhaps I could lay my finger on it, and then again perhaps I couldn't ; but let's talk as if I could. I heard lately that Mr. Haviland (in whose service you have been a good many years, haven't you ?) was looking for this same Samuel Ewart. It is only natural that I should think of obliging him in his turn ; he would be very glad to have news of Samuel Ewart, who died so unfortunately in Jersey."

Reuline paused and looked narrowly at Groult.

He did not want to irritate him too much, but Groult answered quietly:

"If you want to send the certificate to my master you must be quick about it. He is probably dead by now, or not far off."

The old man stuck his tongue in his cheek, and looked at Groult with such evident perspicacity in his green eyes that the latter felt uneasy.

"Poor Mr. Haviland! Well, well, such is life! But you seem very sure that your master will die! It seems, then, one can tell before-hand how certain maladies will end. Well, well, who would have thought it! Now, to return to our business, Mr. Haviland will leave heirs who will certainly be glad to know what has be-come of Samuel Ewart. There is only one thing I want, my good sir, and that is to oblige every-body, if I can."

Groult was quieter now. The wrinkles on his temples seemed to have gathered themselves into a sort of spiteful grin.

"But," he said, "Haviland's heirs won't give you a penny for the paper. You would be a fool to send it to them. What good would it do you? Give it to me; I shall be able to pay you something for it later on."

"Gently, gently. Suppose you explain your little business to me. Daddy Reuline is discretion itself.

When I know what it is all about I will see what is to be done."

" I have nothing to explain to you."

"Oh, good Lord ! I know what's the matter; you are shy. I must help you out. The late Samuel Ewart is put down for a round sum of money in Mr. Haviland's will. Provided as you are, thanks to me, with papers establishing the identity of the defunct legatee, you will find a young man willing, for a consideration, to present himself at the lawyer's office as Samuel Ewart, and receive as such the sum left to him. Good Lord ! don't try to deny it. One must not leave good money idle, and as poor Samuel can't profit by it——

"But, my dear Groult, who is going to answer for the probity of this spurious Samuel Ewart ? Suppose he kept everything for himself ? It would be an indelicate proceeding on his part, and very unpleasant for you. These things have to be considered. There is so much dishonesty in this weary world ! Think it over, be wise. I only want what is for your good."

The old man stuck out the tip of his lizard's tongue and continued :

"I am warning you, and forewarned is forearmed. I know the person who possesses Samuel Ewart's death-certificate   This person is neither a Turk

nor a Jew, wishes you no ill, and is most reason-
able.   And this is what I am authorised to say
to you: Get hold of the legacy, and when you
have got it, offer a decent share of it to this
person, through my intermediary; not half of it—
no, that would be too much, it doesn't do to be
too hard on folks—but something like a bonus of,
well, fifty per cent.   Otherwise this person, quite
contrary to my advice, will insist on making the
document public, and that would be awkward for
you and painful to me."

During this long harangue Groult had quietly
pushed his chair further and further back into
the shadow; now, gathering himself together, he
leapt suddenly on Reuline, and, seizing him by
the throat, cried out:

"Give me the paper, you old Jew, or I will
strangle you!"

He was furious at being thus met by an un-
foreseen obstacle.

Reuline, who was yellow, thin, and dried-up,
and who drew each breath as though it must be
his last, resisted with the strength and suppleness
of a man used to such tussles—his frequent quarrels
with the sailors who pawned their watches with
him for money to get drunk on kept him in good
condition.

Such unexpected resistance only made Groult

more frantic, who saw red, and pulled out his knife; it was a wicked-looking thing, with a pointed blade fastened into a brass-mounted box-wood handle, and was hardly ever out of Groult's hand; he was constantly using it for some purpose or another. The old man, in his struggles to get free, slipped and struck his forehead against the angle of the chimney-piece. Groult, still holding on, fell with him, and saw first a white scratch and then a stream of blood. Reuline's cries and the sight of the blood frightened him, and he lost his head. With singular lucidity he chose his spot and plunged the knife into the old man's breast. Then for a moment, which seemed to him endless, he paid no heed to anything. The man lay under him, resisting still with all his might, his mouth open, his green eyes rolling; then he let go and fell back, opening and shutting his hands convulsively as though trying to grasp something, then suddenly he was still.

His face showed no traces of violent emotion; he seemed to be smiling maliciously in his sleep.

With the end of his knife Groult prised open the lock of the secretary and began to rummage in it, tumbling the papers. The flame of the almost burnt-out candle flickered, and in the midst of the sudden silence the mice ran over the floor. He hunted through packets, portfolios, envelopes, flinging them down, as he finished with them, on to the corpse. Suddenly a bright light sprang up in the room; it was the paper round the candle end which had caught fire. He hunted through old card-board boxes, old blotting-pads, old leather cases, till at last he came on a stamped paper, which he thrust into his pocket with a sigh of relief. He blew out the candle, the wick of which was now floating in melted candle grease, and which, smoking and smelling, flared in his face and scorched his eye-lashes before becoming extinct. He felt about for his cap, and, having found it, went out of the room. He hesitated a moment on the landing before climbing noiselessly up the ladder leading to the attic; here he peered anxiously through the skylight into the street. He could see, by the reflection of the light on the wet pave-ment, that the grocer's shop was not yet shut. Crouching behind some empty boxes, he waited a long time, his legs trembling, his throat dry, his head burning, starting and shivering at the slightest sound. Then, when at last the house and the street were asleep, he crept out, and found a cord with a hook at the end, which the grocer used for hauling bales of goods up into the attic; this he tied to a pulley above the window, and slipped down it with the agility of a monkey.

CHAPTER X

ÉLÈNE had only one idea now that she had passed the convalescent stage, and that was to take possession of René, to hold him to her, and never to leave him. He should be her refuge and her strength. She felt quite certain that her fears would leave her when they were together. She would marry him and would lead a peaceful, warmly-sheltered life between her husband and her father. All her innocent past was bound up in these two men; no bad dream could come gliding over the pillow which she would arrange with so much love.

She knew nothing of the rumours growing and spreading about her in the Quartier.

There were no difficulties made about Mr. Haviland's will; it was opened and read to the heirs by the notary. In it he left his wife, Hélène Haviland *née* Fellaire, all the income accruing from his estate; at her death it was to go to his nephew, George Haviland, or his heirs direct, should he have any.

To Groult was left an annuity of twelve hundred francs.

The testator expressly desired that the personal property of George Haviland, which, he being a minor, his uncle had managed for him, should be entrusted to the care of his old and honourable friend, Mr. Charles Simpson, banker, of Paris.

But Mr. Charles Simpson was suffering from a disease of the spinal cord, caused by a fall from his horse, and therefore could not accept the office his deceased friend had wished to confide to him. Monsieur Fellaire, hearing of this, at once proposed to fill Mr. Simpson's place.

He showed, on divers occasions, the liveliest solicitude for the minor's welfare.

One day after lunch, as he was enjoying his cognac and cigars, he said to his daughter :

" I am as interested in that boy as if he was my own son. In fact, I feel a fatherly affection for him. These sentiments are not under our own control."

Then having piled up a pyramid of sugar in his cup, he went on :

" I really don't know what I would not do for that boy."

He smiled a gentle, melancholy smile as he contemplated the sugar, as though it were the hope, so lovingly conceived, of being useful to George, which he saw melting before his eyes. Then he tossed down the syrup formed by the collapsed pyramid and smiled anew.

Hélène looked at him uneasily; she guessed too well what he was about to propose. He drank a glass of cognac, and said :

"Poor Simpson, that was a most unlucky fall he had ; it shows what weak creatures we all of us are ! A month ago he was full of life and intelligence, and now he is almost idiotic. Perhaps I am exaggerating when I say intelligence ; he never knew how to do business on a large scale ; he was timid, never took any risks."

And Fellaire lighted his cigar with a pompous air ; he knew how to take risks !

Hélène, feeling very uncomfortable, remained silent. Her father, sitting there impassively smoking, in his black clothes, correct and massive, looked in the tobacco smoke like a hero in the clouds— the very apotheosis of a financier.

"Simpson was very cold, very formal," he said ; "I don't know if he would ever have taken a really paternal interest in our George."

Then, incapable of containing himself any longer, he went straight to the point. He dictated a letter to be addressed by Hélène to the family counsel, in which she proposed him as George Haviland's guardian.

Standing up, his head thrown back, his finger pointing commandingly at the page :

" Write, my child, write," he said :

"*I feel assured that this choice would have had the approval of my husband.*"

She hesitated before putting down this colossal lie, but looking at her father, he appeared to her such a worthy figure, with such a tranquil forehead and so calm an air of conviction, that she docilely wrote what he told her.

Fellaire, floating in the serene regions of his imaginary paternity, glowed with good intentions.

He took the letter to the post himself. Hélène, left alone, shuddered with shame and fear—she had betrayed the dead man.

" If he were to come back ! " she thought.

Suddenly she imagined she saw him with frightful distinctness standing before her. His face was absolutely devoid of all expression, so that it was impossible for her to penetrate the mystery of his thoughts. She knew the vision was imaginary, but she could not put it away from her.

.   .   .   .   .   .

Fellaire did not sleep that night. His ideas were working tumultuously under the scarlet handkerchief which served him for a night-cap. He turned over and over, and each time he did so rattled the water-bottle and glass standing on the mahogany

table by the bedside, along with his pipe, his candle-
stick, and his spectacles. The silvery tinkle they
made mingled harmoniously with his thoughts.

The magnificent but honest enterprises, which
would mark his career as a trustee, filled him with
anticipatory admiration. And that was not all. In
his daughter he had a docile capitalist ready to his
hand. He could embark on his great enterprise, the
dream of his life; he could bring forth the child of
his midnight watches, his great work: " The Fiduciary Society for Granting Loans to Wage-earners."

The Government would certainly authorise the
establishment of a society built on a solid basis of
capital. The list of the Board of Directors, who
should be chosen from among titled and decorated
men, would inspire confidence at once.

At this point in his imaginings, Fellaire saw the
terrible ghost of the " Phœnix of the National
Guard " flit across his bed-curtains. He felt a cold
sweat burst out under the triple folds of his bandana,
but he drove away the importunate memory and
plunged again into the contemplation of the future.
He thought of a most effective emblem for " The
Fiduciary "—two hands, emerging from lace cuffs,
and clasping one another. He could already see
this symbolic device printed on the headings of
circulars and prospectuses, engrossed on tickets,
bills of exchange, cheques, shares, stocks, and bank

books, carved in stone, and of immense proportions, decorating the front of the building occupied by "The Fiduciary's" offices, which should be somewhere in the neighbourhood of the new opera-house—for the society would certainly buy a plot of ground and erect a building in a central situation.

The first ray of dawn filtered in through the blinds, and by its light Fellaire could see on his table a pile of unpaid bills from bootmakers and restaurant-keepers.

CHAPTER XI

HE day after the dinner at Bréval's, Longuemare, while lunching at a café, was looking over the newspapers. His eye fell on a column of general information signed "Spectator," a pseudonym he knew Bouteiller used; he frowned as he read the following paragraph:

"Another well known and original figure has disappeared from our midst. Mr. Martin Haviland, whose funeral took place yesterday, has left an odd collection of curiosities in his magnificent hôtel on the Boulevard Latour-Maubourg—some thousands of bottles containing water from all the rivers, streams, brooks, water-courses, fountains, and cascades in the world. Mr. Haviland was as remarkable for his charity as for his collections. His death, which will be much felt by the poor in the Quartier des Invalides, seems to be due to an abuse of belladonna, a drug he took to relieve the acute rheumatism from which he suffered. Such, at least, appears to be the opinion of the medical authorities. We are happy, by the exactness of our information, to be able to reduce this event, so painful in itself, to its rigid proportions."

The last lines of the paragraph threw René into a violent rage. He swore he would mark Bouteiller's face with his riding-whip. "Only I don't even know where the ape lives," he cried impatiently.

He went off to look for him at the offices of what was then the fashionable newspaper, and met him in the vestibule, between the bronze duck and the pink marble pigeon which sat, one on the letter-box and one on the receptacle for manuscripts. The fat reporter was just innocently opening his umbrella (it was raining), and his unconscious air of stupid good-nature disarmed Longuemare. He thought of the days when Bouteiller used to steal his Latin verses from his desk to copy at his leisure, and his heart softened. Bouteiller smiled with delight at sight of him, and cried out:

"Dine with me to-night at Bréval's, old chap; I count on you. Just off to the inauguration of the Grand Rabbi."

Longuemare stopped the way, and, thrusting the crumpled newspaper in his face, asked:

"What is the meaning of the last phrase of your paragraph? Who, to your knowledge, gave undue importance to this affair? Who has been suspected? and of what? Answer me."

Bouteiller stared roundly first at Longuemare, then at the paper, and answered with evident candour:

"I will tell you, my dear fellow. I put that in just to make the par. interesting, that was all; and you see I have kept well within bounds. It is poignant, and yet does not compromise any one. I know what's what. It's understood, then, we meet to-night at Bréval's."

Longuemare turned from him with a shrug of the shoulders. He was shaken by conflicting emotions; his nerves were in a state of intense irritation. He passed from one mood to another—now violent, now sentimental, and felt in the mood for indiscretions. Undoubtedly he was in love with Hélène, and this was beginning to trouble him profoundly.

In the over-excitement imposed on all his faculties by this sentiment, he felt capable of anything. In one week he wrote an article for the *Medical Gazette*, composed his first sonnet, attached himself to a young person who sold flowers in a students' dancing-hall, and spent a quarter's pay on her in eight days. Then suddenly the sonnet, the article, and the flower-seller became equally insipid and uninteresting. He dragged through another dreary week; then one fine day decided that he could now with decency present himself

at the hôtel on the Boulevard Latour-Maubourg,
and offer his condolences to the widow.

It seemed as though a century had passed since
his last visit ; and when he saw the big entrance-
gates, the flight of steps in the courtyard leading
to the hall door, the hall itself with its great
earthenware stove, he felt as old as if he had
lived through several lifetimes.

He waited for some minutes in the drawing-room
before Hélène appeared. She seemed to him to be
taller and paler in her black garments, as if he
now saw her for the first time, yet she had not
really changed much. During her convalescence,
despite her mental tortures, she had become stouter
and her cheeks less hollow ; yet when he looked
at her he felt a delicious sensation of novelty.
Her eyes, under the fair hair which curled on
her forehead, smiled in a vague and charming
manner. She was the first to speak, and the
trivial remark she made thrilled through him ; he
answered inconsequently. She, more mistress of
herself, was secretly pleased at his evident emotion.
He alluded slightly to her recent mourning, and
then by an easy transition began to speak of the
future.

What were his plans ? she asked. He was
going to leave the service, he said, and buy a
practice ; his father would advance him the money.

She approved of this, and suggested the Quartier
Saint James, or the Parc de Neuilly, where she had
several friends to whom she could introduce him.
She promised to consult him herself, and to further
his interests wherever possible. For herself, she did
not know yet what she should do—she no longer
cared for society; she intended to lead a retired life.
Then from a feeling of delicacy, she added that
probably she would not be so well off as people
imagined; she had only the income from Mr.
Haviland's estate, and there were many legacies to
be paid out of it.

"If I become quite poor you won't turn your
back on me?" she asked. Which question he had
the good taste not to answer.

They did not say a word of love, but every look
which passed between them was eloquent. They
breathed heavily, and had the sensation of swimming in a fluid at once suffocating and delicious.
She said she was too hot.

He took her hand in his and held it lightly;
she did not attempt to withdraw it. They were
unconscious of what they did or said, only they
would have gladly died in that supreme moment.
Hélène was the first to break the spell. She took
her hand from his, a shadow passed across her face,
and after a moment she said with a sigh:

"I have done many things which I would not do

again, but I am really better than I have appeared
to be so far."

These words stirred the sleeping waters of
memory, and René turned his head away to hide
the tears that filled his eyes. It was she now who
took his hand. But at that moment a step sounded
in the hall.

"My dear—my dear," she said; and leaving the
phrase unfinished, moved away from him to an arm-
chair, into which she sank.

Fellaire, his entrance announced by the creaking
of his boots, came in. He shook René's hand with
effusion, and began to talk of the old times in the
Rue Neuve des Petits Champs.

"We brought you up, in a way," he said to the
doctor. "We found you—you are our child. Well,
well! you met some curious characters at my
house in those days. It was a good school of
observation for you. And since then you have
travelled and seen many lands, like La Fontaine's
pigeon. Ah, the sea! the sea!" He spoke of
the poetry and the immensity of the ocean, and
became quite emotional, until suddenly recollecting
his letters, he asked permission to open them.

He sat down at a table, spreading himself, his
papers and journals, so as to take up the most
room possible, and went through his correspond-
ence, hissing and growling over it contemptuously

or impatiently, affecting to treat it at one moment
with light disdain, and the next with intensely
concentrated attention.

Hélène and René looked at each other in silence;
they felt as if they two only existed in the world.

Finally Fellaire, after noisily signing his name to
various documents, flung down his pen, and ringing
the bell as though in his own house, gave instructions
for his letters to be posted, and sighed contentedly.
His humour had changed; he was good-natured,
easy, a little inclined to tease. He suggested that
they should go and dine somewhere in the country
—no one need know of it; it would not be exactly
a pleasure trip. They must dine somewhere, why
not have a snack at Meudon?

They all three enjoyed such impromptu excursions.

They found a restaurant at Meudon, with an
arbour overlooking the river.

When Hélène untied her hat-strings, she raised
her arms with a graceful movement that reminded
one of the handles of an amphora. René was filled
with admiration. Her fair curls clustered on her
brow, her eyes shone softly beneath them. They
exchanged a glance so profound and so limpid, it
gave them the sensation of being merged in one
another.

Fellaire, with heavy sighs, talked of the import-

ance of business, and in return for a demand for ink
and paper, was given a little muddy fluid in the
bottom of a bottle, a rusty pen, and a sheet of blue
foolscap, which he covered with figures before
cramming it into his pocket.

Then he brusquely demanded if his young
friend knew any shipowners at Toulon. He rolled
out the word "shipowners" with so much pom-
posity that it seemed as though he had only asked
the question with the intention of producing a
telling effect, which was most probably the case.

At dinner he squeezed half a lemon over his fried
fish with all the grace his fat, short, ring-laden
fingers were capable of.

He contemplated the young couple benignly
through his tortoiseshell spectacles, not without a
secret desire to exhort them and bless them, as in
a melodrama.

Before them, on the river, a landing-stage lay
along the bank; a long narrow island, edged by
a curtain of poplars, cut the horizon line; boats
were passing up and down; women in light summer
gowns moved among the trees, and called in silvery
tones to the occupants of outriggers. The water
blazed with the reflection of the setting sun; then
the light faded from sky and earth, a fresh breeze
sprang up in the sombre verdure, and René put a
black shawl over Hélène's shoulders. Fellaire, who

H

had been telling stories and detailing the ingredients of dishes, unexpectedly began to admire the landscape, and to praise Providence for all its ways. Longuemare answered that Nature presents a scene of eternal carnage, in which everything lives by slaughtering something weaker than itself.

"Now, now, you are exaggerating," said Fellaire.

The shadows were closing round them; but they were all three very happy, and two at least would have stayed on contentedly, had not the business man suddenly remembered the Café de Colmar; it was time to play his game of billiards and to meet his friends, the brokers and advertising agents.

"Children," he said, knitting his thick eyebrows while consulting his watch, "time is flying, and I have an important engagement. Besides, it is going to rain." The wind was rising, driving the clouds furiously across the sky, while a full red moon seemed to be scudding in the opposite direction. They went towards the narrow lane which leads from lower Meudon to the station on the heights. Hélène took René's arm. She walked hesitatingly in the uncertain light, and they were silent; all at once she began to shiver.

"I am frightened," she said.

A tall thin man, with feet disproportionately long, and dressed in rags, started up in front of them.

He pulled off a tattered straw hat, and showed a pale lean face, with two dull hollow eyes. He muttered some sort of a prayer for charity, as he held out his hand.

Hélène pressed closely against René and drew him away.

"Did you see?" she said. "He looked like—oh, I am frightened!"

René himself could not suppress a feeling of uneasiness. The beggar, as a matter of fact, did look like Mr. Haviland; and what made it more painful was that his appearance was so mournful and so dilapidated, he wore such an expression of irremediable suffering, that he suggested the frightful vision of Haviland—not as he used to look, but as he must look then, at that moment.

They climbed on, up the steep path bordered with hedges and walls, the pebbles slipped and rolled under their feet. Hélène stopped to look fixedly at something in the shadow. René could see nothing in front of her but a bed of nettles growing beside a milestone. But the widow saw more than these; she flung up her hands with a loud cry and fell backwards.

Fellaire tried to prop her against the stone. René, who was bending over her, told him to let her lie full length.

She was stiff and motionless. Only her lips

moved, and a little froth gathered at their corners; her eyes stared blankly at the sky.

By-and-by, when she recovered consciousness, she did not seem to think of anything beyond her extreme fatigue. On reaching home, she begged her father to stay the night. She was frightened, she repeated. She gave René her hand—it was limp, lifeless, and icily cold; and she looked at him with an expression of utter hopelessness and discouragement.

CHAPTER XII

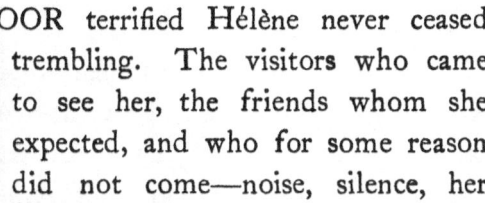OOR terrified Hélène never ceased
trembling. The visitors who came
to see her, the friends whom she
expected, and who for some reason
did not come—noise, silence, her
own apartments, the street itself, everything
frightened her. She started at every encounter.
Her old school friend Cécile, who had married
years before into the money market, came with
much ceremony. Between her airs and graces
and babble, she showed a lurking curiosity which
was torture to Hélène. The paragraph signed
"Spectator" had piqued Cécile's curiosity, but
she almost had to go away without satisfying it.

She was standing up, saying her farewell, when
she thought better of it, and reseated herself.

"These journalists," she said; "they really have
no common sense. What was it one of them said
about the frightful misfortune which had befallen
you, my poor dear? and its just proportions—
proportions? I don't know what one means by
proportions!"

Hélène answered in a scared voice :

" I don't understand you ; I assure you that I am——"

She stopped before committing an irreparable blunder. She was just about to affirm her innocence.

She sent for the number of the journal, and could not sleep after reading it.

In the meantime, a criminal affair had come before the magistrates at Avranches, who were examining into it carefully. A certain Reuline, a pettifogging business agent of somewhat bad reputation, had been found murdered in his lodgings, Rue de Gesvre, Granville. Suspicion first fell on a drunken, debauched longshoreman, who had been to see Reuline about five o'clock the evening before the discovery of the crime. The grocer occupying the ground-floor of the house had seen this man coming down from Reuline's room, evidently in a state of violent excitement. But after a long and careful cross-examination, he was discharged.

Forced to turn his attention to another quarter, the magistrate went over the scene of the crime again. He noticed that the packets of papers which had evidently been taken out of the secretary, turned over rapidly and flung down on the body of the victim, formed several distinct groups—each one was wrapped in a paper envelope, with a name and address written on it. This mass of papers had been prudently left as it was when discovered. The body of the murdered man was drawn from under it with every precaution. One envelope was empty. From its position on the top of the pile, it must have been among those last examined by the assassin. On it was written, "Monsieur Groult, care of Monsieur Haviland, Paris."

The name of Groult was found, not at Granville, but at Avranches, on the register of the Red Horse Inn. Groult was still there, when a warrant was issued against him, and he was arrested.

Hélène, after passing an atrocious night, learnt this piece of news from the papers.

She had seen her husband again; the frightful apparition had reappeared before her. It neither reproached her nor showed signs of hatred or anger ; it merely stood looking at her in the grisly form in which her imagination clothed it. How could she continue to live if it came to her thus every night ?

When her father arrived at lunch-time, she flung herself on him in a delirium of affection and fear ; she lifted supplicating eyes to him ; she held him so tightly that he said :

"Why, what is the matter? You are hurting me."

Then he added that though he had always mistrusted Groult, this was a most unexpected revelation. The wretched man's crime made him shiver; but in the night, he added, he had had an inspiration. He would find Samuel Ewart himself: he had that very morning written to the French Ambassador to England on the subject. He would follow up the search. And as he said it, his eye took on a sharp, keen look which seemed to pierce the ceiling.

It distressed Hélène to see him attaching himself to the dead man's interests.

"Father," she said, "wouldn't you like to go away with your daughter—far, far away?"

"Where?" said he, with busy good-nature. The idea of leaving the Café Colmar seemed to him absurd and monstrous. Recovering his surprise, he kissed Hélène on the brow.

"Baby," he murmured.

Then with his easy and indiscreet kindness, he brought forward a reason which would, he thought, keep the young widow in Paris.

"Our friend Longuemare would be disconsolate if you went away."

She replied gravely that Monsieur Longuemare must only think of marrying some innocent young girl. Then, with clasped hands and in a voice which seemed to come from the very depths of her soul:

"My God, my God! what a pitiless thing life is!"

He took her hands in his, and said in his unctuous, comfortable voice:

"What are you saying? what are you saying, my child?"

Laying his leather portfolio on the table, he lighted a big cigar, wreathed in the smoke of which he proceeded to draw up a memorandum about Samuel Ewart.

From that day Hélène's terror and remorse continually increased, from no external reason, but merely by the workings of her sick brain. The visions became more frequent and more precise. It was difficult for her to distinguish them from reality.

As a result of Groult's cross-examination the magistrate ordered his domicile to be searched. A police commissioner, accompanied by a locksmith, appeared at the hôtel one morning. Madame Haviland was told that he had seized certain papers found in the lodge, and that he asked the favour of a few minutes' interview with the mistress of the house in the course of the next hour or two.

This request fell on Hélène like a blow from a mallet. She distinctly saw her husband in his room, decomposed, but correct, calm, and well satisfied. She saw him seated, turning over the pages of a review tranquilly, as a man who has just returned to his home.

Although his eyes had almost entirely disappeared and were mixed with clay and earth, he noticed a scrap of thread on the table-cloth, and removed it delicately, with the gesture so familiar in his lifetime. Then he vanished.

Hélène was now the prey of new fears. In her ignorance of things she imagined that justice, bent on dragging the confession of her most secret thoughts from her, would hound her on to the same scaffold as the servant Groult. She remembered everything she had read about the execution of Marie-Antoinette; she could feel the cold steel of the executioner's scissors on her neck. The madness of fear took complete possession of her. The rustling of her own dressing-gown made her half faint from fright.

Towards ten o'clock she heard a door bang. She flung open a window, whether with the idea of suicide or escape she did not know. It was only her nephew George returned at his usual time from school. He threw his books impatiently on the table, and, happening to look at his aunt, said :

" How big your eyes are to-day ! "

He then began while waiting for breakfast to

turn over his books, grumbling and pouting because
he had some Greek to prepare. Sitting on the edge
of his chair, one leg tucked under him, his chin
resting on the table, he turned over the leaves of
his dictionary.

He really translated well, in spite of his grimaces,
but he wrote carelessly, blotting his paper, and
licking up the ink with his tongue.

She listened stupidly to the noises from outside, and trembled each time that the boy kicked
his foot against the bars of his chair. He was
imitating the grave, affected voice of his professor.

"You will notice, gentlemen, the harmony of
Sophocles' verses. We don't know how to pronounce them; we pronounce them all wrong, but
still what harmony! Monsieur Labrunière, you
will conjugate the verb δίδωμι ten times. Yes,
what harmony!"

Then in his own squeaky voice:

"Auntie, I swear to you that my professor wears
paper collars. We call him Python; do you know
why? One day he said: 'Gentlemen, Python was
a monster of repulsive ugliness and malignant spite-
fulness'; and Labrunière whispered, 'Just like you.'
Labrunière is awfully funny. Do you know, Auntie,
you are really a very pretty woman?" At last he
fixed his wandering mind on the Greek text, which
he went over, word by word, like a magpie, filling

the room with his high-pitched tones, calling out the lines as he wrote them down, and stopping every now and then to count his marbles.

"Κάρα θεῖον, the divine head, Ἰοκάστης of Jocasta, τέθνηκε is dead. (How stupid this is!) She went—πρὸς τὰ νυμφικὰ λέχη, towards the nuptial couch, which means the bedroom. You notice, gentlemen, what a happy expression! how harmonious! κόμην σπῶσ', tearing her hair; καλεῖ, she calls; Λάϊον, Laïus; νεκρόν, dead. You see, Auntie, in French a laïus means a sermon, but in Greek it means an old fellow whom Jocasta had married, and the marriage had not turned out happily. *Tearing her hair she calls the dead Laïus.*

From these scraps of Greek and French Hélène could make out an antique and noble story of a woman's despair.

George hurried on, eager to get to the end.

"Κρεμαστὴν τὴν γυναῖκ' ἐσείδομεν, we saw the woman hanged." He signed his initials at the bottom of the paper, stuck out his tongue, all violet with ink, and chanted, "Hanged! hanged! I've finished."

Hélène rose and went to her room. She was so calm, so precise, so certain of what she had to do; she seemed like a statue of Necessity.

Wrapped in her black shawl and her widow's veil, she went down the servants' staircase.

CHAPTER XIII

HEN she reached the street she staggered, dazzled by the brilliant morning sunshine, in which every object showed with extreme clearness. The carriages, the trees, the kiosks of the news-vendors, the most distant passers-by were all so distinctly outlined despite their smallness that they appeared close at hand. The light was painful to her; she saw everything with unconscious eyes. The most insignificant things, such as the numbers on the cabs and the names over the shops, engraved themselves on her vision in such minute detail as to be fatiguing to her worn nerves; they seemed to strike at her and wound her. She would have gone back, but she could not stop; all power of reflection had left her. A living woman had never before been so empty of thought. An idea had come to her, so simple, clear, and definite, it excluded all others. She walked on not even aware that she was walking, feeling as if she were flying and yet very weak, possessed only by this idea, incapable of a voluntary effort.

A little girl trotted in front of her carrying a
baby and a bottle of milk. She watched the
white drops as they fell one by one on the pavement; all the mental faculty that remained to her
fixed itself on the spilt milk. Each drop that
splashed over gave her a feeling as of physical
pain.

When she reached the quays the freshness of
the wide, open space, the effect of the light on
the water, and the cool breeze from the river,
drew a sigh from her.

She hesitated a moment, then, turning to the
right, went on. The Quai d'Orsay was perfumed
with the scent of flowers in the neighbouring
gardens. A stream of omnibuses, cabs, business
men, and agile work-girls pouring from the Rue
du Bac to the Pont Royal stopped her for a few
seconds. She crossed the bridge without looking
at the water, and, turning again to the right, went
down the steps to the shore, where, by a group
of willow-trees, the floating baths were moored.
She passed over the plank and on to the boat,
which smelt of hot water and tar.

She waited quietly, biting the top of her parasol,
while the white-aproned attendant prepared her
bath; and went quietly into the cabin, saying
she would ring when she wanted her bath-robe.

As soon as the little door closed behind her

she drew back the calico curtains with an impatient gesture, and, opening the window, leant out, breathing deeply. The Seine flowed beneath with little shining ripples. From the washerwomen's boat moored on the opposite bank came the muffled sound of their wooden beaters. A buzz of voices rose above the men's enclosure at the side.

She looked on the bright scene with an indifferent, almost happy eye. With her black cashmere shawl drawn tightly round her shoulders, her widow's veil flung back over her bonnet and floating like a funereal cloud about her head, she was more beautiful than she had ever been. Her whole being seemed to exhale a voluptuous calm.

The screw of a steamer splashed as it drew near. The floating bridge of the bathing establishment oscillated slightly, and a steamer going to Point du Jour passed so close to her she could hear the voices of the passengers. Two vulgar-looking young men leaning over the side eyed her boldly, thinking, no doubt, of the toilet she was going to lay aside.

She noticed them, and she heard the elder of the two, who was fair and had red patches on his cheeks, say:

"What a pretty woman! One wouldn't mind——"
But the boat had passed; the funnels were already

being lowered under the arches of the Pont Royal.

Was it disdain or satisfaction that raised the corners of her mouth in a slight smile? She was calm; her eyes wandered quietly from one point to another without betraying the slightest uneasiness. She raised her pretty arms with a graceful gesture which would have fascinated more than one man, and passed her hand across her brow; then she closed the window, evidently indifferent to all she saw from it.

It was noon-day.

Two o'clock came, and she had not rung. At ten minutes past two the attendant, surprised at not having been called, opened the door of the cabin and asked if Madame needed anything.

There was no one in the bath, but opposite it, between the window and the looking-glass, a tall, dark figure hung.

The girl fled shrieking for help.

Hélène Haviland had hanged herself with one of her nephew's neckties to a clothes'-hook. She was wearing round her shoulders the shawl which René had wrapped her in a month before in the arbour at Meudon. Her knees were stiff, and the tips of her boots touched the floor. The body was leaning to the left against a chair, which had no doubt been placed there on purpose. The face was covered with her widow's veil. When this was raised, the face showed congested; the tongue, black and swollen, protruding from the mouth.

When the police commissioner appeared on the scene he remarked:

"Well, I have seen many women who have committed suicide; but this is the first I have seen who has hanged herself."

CHAPTER XIV

LONGUEMARE was profoundly grieved at the hideous and ill-omened end of the woman he loved, though at first he did not appear overcome by it. He worked furiously at his profession; but he grew sombre, hard, and brutal. He showed none of his good qualities, save his zeal and intelligence as a surgeon. Quarrelsome with his companions, cynical with women, he wore out the most patient of his friends, and they left him alone. His irritability reached such a pitch he could not take a meal in his *crèmerie* without disputing with the waiters, the landlord, or the young lady behind the counter.

A somewhat brusque observation from the head physician at the hospital caused him to send in his resignation, and one fine day he arrived unexpectedly at his father's house, in the depths of the Ardennes, without books, clothes, or linen, a three-weeks'-old beard and a sulky air.

The land surveyor was a little, dried-up, old man, who pruned his trees, bottled his wine, cemented the dilapidated tiles in the flooring of the rooms, chopped his firewood, and came and went, always busy and always interested in the smallest details of life. He shrugged his shoulders when he saw his son lying all the day long in the garden, an empty pipe in his mouth, and a tattered straw-hat on his head.

One day after dinner he confided to René that he had " a lump on his arm " ; it did not hurt him, but seemed to increase in size. " What must he do for it ? " he asked.

" Nothing," replied René, turning his back on the indignant old man.

With his pruning-knife or scissors in his hand, he would often pause, as though by chance, near the heap of hay on which his son sprawled for hours at a time.

" If you are ill, why don't you go to bed ? " he would say; or, " If any one comes, I beg you in your own interests to change your clothes."

René acquired a habit of going out after each meal. A little river ran by the garden, and he would lie down among the rushes which grew on its banks. He did not indulge in day-dreams. Everything appeared to him to be painful, absurd. and hard ; his grief had no charm, no beauty. He remained in this state for several weeks.

One day, as he was yawning stupidly at the water's edge, he saw some naked children, gliding with

clumsy but pretty movements from one stone to
another, in the bed of the river. These little creatures, with their yellow hair, and rosy, laughing
faces, calling, screaming, tumbling over one another,
splashing about in the water, gave a joyous note to
the dreary landscape. Longuemare called out to
them on a sudden impulse, but they scuttled off,
clinging on to the mossy stones by their hands
and knees, diving to the muddy bottom, and not
making much progress. One of them crawled into
the crevice of an overhanging rock, where he
thought he was safely hidden; but René caught
him, and plucked him out of his hole like an
eel. He could not have looked very cross, for
the child was not frightened.

"Listen to me, you little savage," said the
surgeon. "If you will bring me some frogs, I
will give you a bright new penny. You know how
to catch frogs? I live over there at old Longuemare's house."

When he got the frogs he stayed in his room,
which soon began to smell strongly of chemicals
and tobacco. Daddy Longuemare would look up
from weeding his borders, to the little window,
outside which hung bunches of mutilated frogs
strung on wires. He felt a sort of religious
respect for his son, now that he was working. He
took up as small a space as possible in the house,

and moved about on the tips of his toes. He
forbade the servant to go into René's room while
he was at work there, even to make the bed.

One day at table, as he was peeling a pear, he
asked his son:

"Couldn't I help you prepare your frogs?
Wouldn't you like me to cut you some little boards,
for instance? I could paint them, and gum a layer
of fine sand on them for you."

"Gum fine sand on little boards? What on earth
for?"

The father explained that he thought his son was
making artistic groups of stuffed frogs.

"I have seen them most cleverly arranged," he
said, "in the naturalists' shops in Paris, some of
them had wooden swords, and were supposed to be
fighting duels; some of them were playing piquet
with miniature packs of cards, and some were sitting
in an arbour, drinking out of doll's glasses. They
were most ingenious. I thought, my boy, you were
doing things of that kind?"

He was much disappointed when he heard his
son was only making experiments, which in his eyes
were child's play, only fit for schoolboys. From
that moment his face resumed its anxious expression; and when, looking up from the garden, he
perceived the frogs at the window, he would shake
his head in a pitying manner.

One day René told him he was going away. When the two men said good-bye they assumed, each one, a gruff, off-hand tone of voice, an impassive visage and a stiff attitude; they separated with sullen firmness.

But the old man was weeping into his check handkerchief as he returned home, and his son, stretched on the bench of a third-class carriage, wiped his eyes as he filled his pipe.

At Reims two young fellows, shopmen apparently, got into the carriage. One of them was reading the *Petit Journal*, and telling the other the important bits of news.

"The ministerial crisis continues.—Great excitement caused at Gros-Caillou by an explosion.—The man Groult (Juste Desiré) was executed at six o'clock this morning, on the market-place at Granville."

"What had he done?" asked the friend.

"He murdered an old man. He was accused also of having poisoned a rich Englishman, but the second crime was not proved at the trial. Don't you remember the Groult affair?"

"No," said the other; then after a moment's silence:

"Does it give any details?"

"'At four o'clock this morning the fatal engine,'" he read in a low voice—Longuemare did not catch the rest; and the owner of the newspaper, folding it up, said: "Up to the last moment he declared that the murder of his victim was not premeditated. All the same, he was an awful scoundrel. . . . I could do with a snack, couldn't you?"

In Paris, Longuemare lived in a state of dull torpor. He had still a few hundred francs left from his pay in Cochin-China, so there was no immediate need for him to work. He rose at noon and went to the Luxembourg Gardens, where he would sit on a bench among the whirling leaves the autumn wind brought down. He would hold his head till his hands left their marks on his cheeks. The first cold weather made him seem more listless and heavy. He dragged through his days in the stifling atmosphere of some little café, without even reading the papers or playing billiards.

One day in spring he met an old acquaintance— Nouilhac, a big heavy fellow, a sort of half-peasant, whose father, a farmer in Auvergne, had left him a stocking full of money, which he spent with the appetite of a glutton and the stinginess of a serf; but as he was now approaching forty years of age, he was becoming more serious.

He had bought, in his own part of the country, a forgotten thermal spring, with its mouldy establishment, and was planning how to get visitors to it.

His pockets were full of bottles of mineral water, and prospectuses illustrated with vignettes showing Roman baths and a sixteenth-century piscina, copied from some old engravings. Offering a bottle to Longuemare, he said :

"Hot springs containing sulphur, chlorine, soda, arsenic, and iodo-bromine, and naturally effervescent."

Then he told a long tale about it.

The establishment was thirty miles from Clermont, on the border of a lake, at the foot of a superb basaltic mountain. The population of the village consisted of fifteen or twenty goat-herds and thirty goitrous men and women.

Nouilhac had inherited from his father three of four tumble-down dwellings in the same village, which, repainted and repaired, could be turned into cottages for visitors. The Hôtel de César opposite the baths could accommodate from thirty to forty people. Later on, a casino might be added. They must go slowly at first, but who could say what the future would bring forth. Finally, he asked Longuemare to join him. "Come," said he ; "you can be the doctor attached to the establishment."

He had a deep respect, inspired by the unanimous opinion of their common friends, for the medical talents of the ex-army surgeon. All Longuemare's comrades admitted that he possessed the eye and hand of a master.

His answer to Nouilhac was :

" Your baths are in a hole. No one will ever come to them, except perhaps a few scrofulous and scabby individuals, who will get worse there. If I go, it will be to stay the winter as well as the summer."

He accepted, without disputing, the small salary Nouilhac offered. The latter considered that the doctor of the establishment would be well paid by the large international practice he was bound to make among the foreign visitors.

Longuemare spent the next day running about Paris buying the few clothes, books, and instruments he needed. Towards six o'clock in the evening, as he was coming down the Avenue des Champs-Élysées, he stopped before a Punch and Judy show. A triple row of idlers was pressing against the cord which, passed round the trunks of the trees, enclosed a space reserved for paying spectators. Behind these, small children with discouraged faces peeped between the legs of a soldier and their nurse's skirts.

A little apart from the crowd stood a bent heavy, unhealthily fat old man, whose wan face wore an expression of desolate inertia. He was dressed in a frock-coat—too short behind and too long in front —so shabby, it was rubbed yellow at the collar and wrists. He was looking at the Punch and Judy show, or rather kept his eyes in that direction, for his look floated vaguely between sky and earth.

At the sight of Monsieur Fellaire de Sisac, Longuemare felt much moved; all his fond recollections came surging to the surface of his soul.

Fellaire shook his hand, and tried to say something, but could not find words. Longuemare, with a kind of brusque tenderness and pity, said:

"Come—come along with me."

"It just happens that I can," answered Fellaire; "I have no business to do this evening."

He was living in the Rue Truffaut, in the wilds of Batignolles, he said; and added, "It is not very central, but with the trams——"

Was it a day, or a hundred years, since they had last met they wondered, as they sat facing each other in a smoky restaurant in the Rue Montmartre.

They did not speak of her, but both saw her, in imagination, beside them.

When they were eating nuts after dinner, Longuemare told de Sisac about his plans for going to Mont-Dore, and what he was going to do there, adding quite simply:

"I am going to take you with me."

The old man, rolling his startled eyes, cried out:

"What! leave Paris! It isn't possible. One can only live in Paris—and then my business?"

Pitiful though it was, Longuemare could not help smiling.

"Come with me, there will be plenty for you to do. You will be the inspector, controller, registrar."

These titles struck de Sisac's fancy, and he declared that "he was willing to give his adhesion to an enterprise that, and for which—in short, if his experience could be of any use."

They made an appointment to meet next day. Longuemare, as he recrossed the bridge, said to himself:

"I can't help it; I keep thinking that he is my father-in-law."

.   .   .   .   .   .

The first season at the Baths was fairly successful. Some Russians, and a French family from Lyons, came to Nouilhac's establishment. Fellaire stood about near the spring and tasted the water from time to time with a knowing air. His occupation was not very distinctly defined. Nouilhac would certainly not have engaged him but for Longuemare, and it was with the latter's money that he paid him.

"Let him think that you are giving him a salary," the doctor said; "and above all, don't let him think that it is mine he is drawing. I can manage for myself."

He gave a few consultations to the Russians, and was occasionally called into the mountains to see some peasant who had sprained his ankle while on a Sunday spree.

The visitors left with the swallows—not in a flock as they did, but in couples, or alone, one after the other.

The winter came. Snow covered the valley. On the jagged black granite rocks, and on the coloured marble slabs, ice hung in stalactites. The pine trees in the ravines loomed like phantoms, big and shadowy through the mist. The horizon was closed in by a sea of darkness.

In the thermal establishment, the old-fashioned red and brown paint peeled off in flakes. Fellaire de Sisac played dominoes all day long with the landlord in the lower floor of the Hôtel de César, and Longuemare sat, his feet on the fire-dogs, smoking his pipe. From time to time he would feel the pulse in his left wrist with his right thumb, and murmur to himself in a low voice:

"Fever, tension, and acute pain in the hypochondriac region—cough, oppressed breathing, sympathetic pain in the right shoulder; nothing is wanting. I have developed a fine hepatic disease."

And he smiled, for the first time for a year four months and six days.

THE FAMISHED CAT

THE FAMISHED CAT

CHAPTER I

OR three days the November winds had been whipping the populous faubourg, now clothed in the first shadows of night. Puddles of water shone under the gas-lamps. A black mud, churned by the steps of men and horses, covered the road and the pavement. Workmen with their bags of tools on their shoulders, women returning from the cook-shop with portions of beef between two plates, scurried with bent backs before the rain with the sullen stolidity of beasts of burden.

Monsieur Godet-Laterrasse, tightly buttoned up in his black clothes, toiled with the populace along the muddy way leading to the top of Montmartre. Monsieur Godet-Laterrasse carried his head high under his umbrella, which, much dilapidated by many bygone storms, fluttered in the wind like the wing of a big wounded bird. His jaw being prominent and his forehead receding, it was easy for his face to assume a horizontal attitude; so that his

eyes, without his troubling to raise them, could see
the sooty sky through the holes in the silk.   Walking, now with feverish haste, now with dreamy
slowness, he turned into a dark and filthy alley,
edged along the wall covered with mouldy trellis-
work, which surrounded a bathing establishment,
and after a moment's hesitation entered an eating-
house, where men, dressed like himself in torn and
shabby black clothes, were silently feeding in a
terrible atmosphere; the warm greasy odour of
which was rendered further obnoxious by a repulsive smell of wet flannel costumes coming from the
neighbouring baths.

Monsieur Godet-Laterrasse bowed to the lady at
the desk in his peculiar manner, flinging his head
back with a grave smile.   Then, having hung up
his shining and battered top-hat, he sat down before
a smeary marble table and smoothed his hair with
the gesture which usually accompanied his meditation.   The gas burnt with a hissing sound and fell
full on the man's woolly hair and his mulatto face;
the skin, with its colour half washed out by the
snows and rains of European winters, looked dirty,
as did also his wrinkled hands with their flat nails,
marked at the ends by milky crescents.   Without
calling the waiter, without even looking towards the
desk, he drew a newspaper from his pocket and
began to read it in an audible voice.   He hardly

stopped to eat the calf's-head, of which portions had already been served to the other silent and resigned guests.

Having eaten, they faded away one after the other into the darkness and rain. Only one, toothless and gloomy, lingered over his dried raisins. The mulatto having emptied his decanter, at the bottom of which was a deposit of lees and crust, wiped his mouth, folded his napkin, put his paper in his breast pocket with the air of a wrestler closing with his adversary, got up, took down his hat, and made towards the door. He was just stepping into the wet night when a small, purple-faced, oily man came out of a side door, grubby with greasy finger-marks, and limped into the dining-room. Monsieur Godet-Laterrasse saluted the restaurant-keeper with one of his backward bows.

"Good-evening, Monsieur Godet," said the fat man. "This is bad weather we are having, and it does a deal of harm! By the way, Monsieur Godet, if you could give me something on account to-morrow, I should be much obliged. I am not the man to worry you, as you know very well, but I have a heavy payment to make at the end of the week."

Monsieur Godet-Laterrasse replied in an accent at once oratorical and infantine, without pronouncing the r's, that there was money owing to him, that he

K

would draw on his editor next day without fail, that
he could not think how he had come to neglect the
eating-house keeper's bill, but it was a mere trifle,
anyway.   The fat man, who did not seem dazzled
by these promises, answered in a drawling tone:

"Don't forget, Monsieur Godet.   Good-night,
Monsieur Godet."

And Godet-Laterrasse disappeared in his turn in
the darkness streaked with rain, which had already
swallowed up the last lean diner in Bather's Alley.
All the ways of the world were open before him.
He took that leading up the hill, which the tempest
was besieging and drowning in a determined deluge.
A blast of wind did its best to carry the mulatto
off his feet, a traitorous gust turned his umbrella
inside out.   Monsieur Godet-Laterrasse re-estab-
lished the concavity of this domestic apparatus, but
the silk, split in every part, floated like a black
flag on the denuded framework.   Under this grotesque and sinister standard he climbed up the steep
steps of the Passage Cotin, which had now become
a mountain torrent.   He could hear nothing but the
splashing of his footsteps, and the mysterious utterances of the wind.   Invisible to all but himself,
the vague shadows of an editor and a newspaper
manager fled before him in the distance.   He went
up eighty steps, and stopped at a little door, over
which was a lantern hanging from a creaking cord

and winking like a diseased eye. Entering the house, he stole furtively past the concierge's lodge.

A rapping against the partition called him back. He opened the glass door in an agony of apprehension. A shrill and sexless voice coming from an alcove informed him there was a letter for him on the chest of drawers. He took the letter, and going down six sticky stairs entered his room. As soon as he had lit a candle he examined the envelope suspiciously.

The post had not brought him anything pleasant for many a long day. But, when he broke the seal and began to read, his white teeth flashed out in a half smile. His childish nature, withered by poverty, brightened at the smallest piece of luck. At that moment he was glad to be alive. He turned out his pockets, and scraped together a little tobacco dust, mingled with crumbs and bits of fluff; this he stuffed into a short pipe, then he slipped voluptuously between the dirty ¡sheets of his sofa-bed, and began to chant in a low voice the words of the letter which had so delighted him :

"DEAR SIR,—I am passing through Paris with my son Remi, whom I have brought up from Brest, where he has been at school. I thought you might prepare him for his degree. In education, as in

everything, I am all for advanced ideas.   Will you
breakfast with us to-morrow, Saturday, at eleven
o'clock, at the Grand Hotel, when we can perhaps
come to some arrangement ?—Faithfully yours,

"A. SAINTE-LUCIE."

Monsieur Godet-Laterrasse, having finished chant-
ing the letter, lighted his pipe and wrapped himself
in smoke and dreams.   What a caress of Fortune
was this unexpected letter !   He had met Sainte-
Lucie in Paris towards the end of the Empire, at
the house of some prominent democratic personage,
and had even received a visit from him.

"It was," thought the mulatto, "at the time
that I was writing articles for the *Grand Universal
Encyclopædia.*   I was living in a fine furnished room
in a hotel in the Rue de Seine.   I must have my
amiable visitor's card somewhere still."   Stretching
out his thin brown arm he reached an old cigar
box full of papers from the mantelpiece, and began
to rummage in it.

The slowly accumulated contents of a drawer
had doubtless been emptied bodily into the box
at the time of some removal, for the papers on
the top were the oldest.   An envelope which he
opened only recalled distant and confused souvenirs.
"Ah !" he thought, "this is from my poor brother,
the coffee merchant at Saint Paul.   He was not

attracted to Paris; he was not wrought upon as I was by ideas," and he read out haphazard:

"You must have learnt from the newspapers that a cyclone has passed over Bourbon Island and destroyed all the plantations. So I have gone into guano. And you? are you still writing rot for Parisian rags?"

"Unhappy man! unhappy man!" murmured Godet-Laterrasse. Leaning on his pillow he opened another letter in the same writing and read once more:

"I can't send you any money, because, coffee having fallen, I had to invest all my available capital while the market was glutted with low-priced products. I did a magnificent stroke of business. You will understand, therefore, that it is impossible for me to send you any money. Durand, who has just returned from Paris, tells me that you are still going in for public meetings and riots on the boulevards. You will get your head broken one of these days, and your friends will say you belonged to the secret police. When you are tired of playing the fool, come back to Bourbon. You can keep my shop; it is a lazy man's work which will suit you perfectly."

"Keep his shop! what blasphemy," cried Monsieur Godet-Laterrasse.

And he flung aside the impious letter. The

bottom of the box was full of invitations to non-religious funerals, judgment summonses, bills, and cuttings from newspapers. One of these, on the back of which was a pedicure's advertisement, illustrated by a bare foot on a stool, he read with a smile :

"One of our most valiant spirits, one of our most hardy pioneers of progress, Monsieur Godet-Laterrasse, a creole from Réunion Island, is putting the finishing touches to his great book, ' The Regeneration of Society by the Black Races.'   One of the principal chapters of this important work is to appear immediately in *The Literary Funnel*."

"Alas !" thought Godet-Laterrasse, "just as the chapter was about to appear *The Literary Funnel* died.   How many journals perish thus in the flower of their youth !"

At last he found among a handful of visiting cards the one he was looking for.   He considered it attentively and read it over :

ALIDOR SAINTE-LUCIE

BARRISTER

Formerly Minister of Public Instruction, and of the Navy, Member of the Chamber of Deputies, President of the Haïtian Artistic Commission

GRAND HOTEL, PARIS

And, in the midst of the smoke which filled the room, Godet-Laterrasse saw a vision of the gigantic mulatto arriving from Haïti, all smiles and money. He blew out the candle and went to sleep.

His dreams were peopled with spectres. The shade of the restaurant-keeper in Bather's Alley advanced limping towards him, and said, in a terrifyingly gentle voice, "Don't forget me, Monsieur Godet."

It was nearly nine o'clock, and it was still raining, when the first streak of day entered the room : when it did come, it was only the disgusting reflection of a dirty borrowed light. The room had no other outlook than on to the wall propping up the neighbouring house, a house which, with its five plaster storeys, overlooked all the roofs in the passage. This rugged bulging wall, cracked, broken, green, and sweating, was terminated by the brickwork balcony of an Italian terrace five or six yards higher than Godet-Laterrasse's room, which it clothed in eternal shadow. The window was separated from the wall by a boggy alley, two yards wide, strewn with salad leaves, egg-shells, and the remnants of paper kites.

When the mulatto awoke, he looked at the dripping window-panes, picked up his heavy boots, which had left a damp mark on the floor, and put them on regretfully. Then, having finished his austere toilet, he seized the ruins of his umbrella, and left the room.   A confused grumbling met him as he passed the concierge's lodge.

"I have not forgotten your little bill, Madame Alexandre," he said.

He mounted the ten topmost steps of the Passage Cotin, and walked, in a river of mud, past the desolate façade of the Swiss Chalet, and the stone yards of the Votive Church.   At the bottom of the Rue Lepic he stopped short, so as not to walk over two bits of straw which formed a cross on the pavement, in front of a packer's shop. Having avoided this danger (for he was sure that to walk over a cross would bring him ill luck), his lofty mood returned to him, and with his magnificent head thrown back again he continued on his way, an intellectual conqueror, towards the heart of Paris, carrying high the eight-pointed framework of his dilapidated umbrella, which looked like the complicated weapon of a savage warrior.

CHAPTER II

ONSIEUR ALIDOR SAINTE-
LUCIE, son of a rich merchant of
Port-au-Prince, studied for the law
in Paris, and returned to Haïti to
be present at the coronation of Soulouque, crowned emperor under the name of
Faustin I. As a coloured man, and a man of
means, he had everything to fear from his black
Majesty. He went bravely ahead in the face of
danger, and made himself remarked in the imperial
palace by his zeal in upholding the sovereign's
policy. Appointed Attorney-General at the imperial court of Port-au-Prince, he had a few of
his fellow-citizens shot, quite unmaliciously. He
accepted from the emperor the office of Minister
of Public Instruction, and of the Navy; then,
thinking that he perceived a secret but energetic
opposition springing up against him, he took a
holiday, and made a trip to France.

From Paris he wrote letters warmly supporting
the revolution which put an end to the sanguinary
gaieties of the black empire, and returned to Haïti

to be elected member of the Chamber of Deputies. His first act in the Assembly was to introduce a measure proposing to erect an expiatory monument to the memory of the victims of tyranny. Certainly, the least that the former Attorney-General could do for some of these victims, was to give them a tomb.

The project was taken into consideration, the proposition carried, and the citizen, Alidor Sainte-Lucie, was made president of the commission charged with the execution of this national work. Monsieur Alidor quite understood the advantage which this presidentship conferred on him. Whenever there was any shooting going on in the island he took out a passport and went to Paris to get new plans for the monument. He adored Paris because of its little theatres and its political cafés. At the end of twenty years the artistic commission was still in full activity.

Monsieur Alidor Sainte-Lucie was a very handsome mulatto, with an immense athletic frame. He carried his copper-coloured face proudly, and had, in spite of his flat nose, a grand air, especially since his hair, retreating from his brow, had left it shining like bronze. He made no attempt to disguise his age, and wore his grizzled beard clipped close. Very particular about his personal appearance, he affected white waistcoats and patent leather shoes, and saturated himself with heavy, sickly perfumes.

Thus well dressed and scented, his powerful figure showing off well in clothes of faultless English cut, he walked up and down his room at the Grand Hotel, waiting for the tutor, while his son drew caricatures on the cover of a book, and a waiter laid a table for three persons, near the fire.

Sketches, models, plaster casts, sepia drawings, photographs, and plans of every sort for the commemorative monument to the victims of tyranny, lay about and encumbered the furniture. On a side table was a little pyramid of painted plaster covered with gilded palms; on the secretary stood a terra-cotta column surmounted by a sort of winged monkey, with the following inscription on the pedestal: " *To the Genius of Black Liberty.*" A photograph on the chimney-piece in front of the mirror represented a negress standing before a sarcophagus, on which she was depositing a roll of paper bearing these simple words: "*Artistic Commission; Monsieur Sainte-Lucie, president.*" Nothing more!

On the ground was a half-open hand in cast iron, a gigantic hand emerging from a curtain-like sleeve. A label hung from the wrist: " *Portion of Design No.* 17, *full size, E.D.*"

Three little golden brown rolls lay on the table-napkins. Monsieur Sainte-Lucie looked at the clock. Perhaps the crisp glazed crust of the bread aroused his appetite, or perhaps he was afraid of being kept waiting; his sleepy eyes, which a few moments before had shone so gently under their somewhat distended lids, suddenly flashed with a wild light. They softened again, however, when Godet-Laterrasse appeared in the doorway. As the waiter held back the curtain, one saw first a chin with an Adam's apple showing prominently above a white cotton cravat. Godet-Laterrasse bowed.

"My son, Remi," said Sainte-Lucie, presenting the young man, who, consenting to leave his unfinished sketch, came forward with a lazy swagger.

He was a handsome boy, with a pure olive complexion, who rolled his big, bored-looking eyes, and seemed to open his great sensual mouth at random.

When they sat down, Monsieur Sainte-Lucie took up twice as much room as Monsieur Godet-Laterrasse. The mulatto from Haïti was of a warm, golden tone, which appeared richer still when contrasted with the other's which seemed to have been smeared with soot and then badly washed. The mulatto from Bourbon was weak-looking, rumpled, and muddy; but his naïvely pompous expression, and his childish pride, inspired the kind of pity one feels for a learned dog or an unfortunate genius.

The affair which brought them together was broached between the devilled kidneys and the green peas. It was Godet-Laterrasse who opened the question.

"Well, my friend," said he, tapping his future pupil on the shoulder, "so we are going to take our degree at the old university?"

Monsieur Alidor rose to the bait and said, crumbling his bread nonchalantly:

"As I wrote to you, my dear Godet—and, by-the-bye, I had a great deal of trouble to find your address. It was Brandt—you know Brandt, the tailor—who discovered it by the merest chance; it seems he was looking for you also."

"It is quite possible," said Godet-Laterrasse, making a movement as though to brush something away.

"As I wrote to you, I am counting on you to prepare this scamp here for his degree, and to make a man of him."

Monsieur Godet-Laterrasse braced himself against the back of his chair till his head was almost horizontal, and said:

"Before we go further, my dear Sainte-Lucie, I must make my profession of faith. My principles are unshakable. I am a man of iron, whom you may break, but you cannot bend."

"I know, I know," said Sainte-Lucie, as he continued to crumble his bread.

" The education which I shall give your son will be essentially a liberal education."

" I know, I know."

" It is a civic degree which I shall ensure our Remi winning gloriously. In preparing him for it, I shall consider not so much the candidate for university honours as the legislator of the Haïtian Republic. After all, what does that pedantic old witch of a university matter to me ? "

The former Minister, who was a practical as well as an eloquent man, signed to him with his eyebrows not to talk in this way before his pupil; but the liberal preceptor, carried away by the sublimity of his personal ideas, went on :

"The university means monopoly, the university means routine, the university represents the enemy ! Down with the university ! " Then laying his hand on the arm of the young man, who seemed too indifferent to be surprised : " My friend, if I prepare you to take your degree, I shall teach you the primordial truths ; so that when, on leaving my hands, you present yourself before the examiners at the Sorbonne, you will be their judge rather than they yours. You can say to the Caros and the Taillandiers, ' I have principles, and you have none. It is that man of iron, it is Godet-Laterrasse, who has formed my mind.' Ha ! these fine gentlemen will know who I am some day ! "

During this speech young Remi was tranquilly occupied in surreptitiously extracting lumps of sugar from the basin and slipping them into his pocket.

Monsieur Alidor, who was naturally inclined to appreciate eloquence, thought this method of preparing for an examination was fine, but a little perilous. As he was naturally very obstinate, however, he did not give up the idea of confiding his son to the creole from Bourbon.

"Remi," he said, carelessly drawing a louis from his pocket, "go and get some cigars downstairs. Say that they are for me."

Left alone with his guest, he continued to crumble his bread silently. He had a special way of holding his tongue, which was mysterious and imposing. Then, in the gentle voice of a man sure of his own strength, he pointed out to the future preceptor that it was a question of working to pass the examinations—an essentially practical enterprise; that the programme must be followed to the letter; and that, as a matter of fact, Greek and Latin were of more importance than primordial truths.

"Certainly, certainly," replied the man of iron.

Asked if he had had any experience of teaching, his reply was vague.

They then came to the question of money.

The former Minister asked the tutor to accept

a monthly salary of two hundred francs; but Godet-Laterrasse refused to consider this baga-telle, with an indignant shake of the head.

Remi came back with the cigars, followed by a slight good-looking man whose golden beard swept his chest. He did not take off the small soft hat he wore on the back of his head like a cap.

"You are welcome, Labanne," said Sainte-Lucie, without rising to greet him. "Will you have a cigar?"

Labanne's only answer was to take an amber-mounted meerschaum pipe and a tobacco-pouch with the arms of Brittany from his pocket. He walked round the room, looking with the air of a connoisseur at the photograph on the mantelpiece. Finally he threw a side-glance at the terra-cotta column.

"Who," said he, "is the joker who furnished you with this model of a stove-pipe?" Then, affecting to be interested in the gilded pyramid, he closed his eyes and said: "They have forgotten the slit to put the pennies through." As the others did not understand, he added: "Of course, the thing was meant for a money-box."

"What can I do? I take what is given me," said Sainte-Lucie philosophically. "You haven't brought your design, have you, Labanne?"

"I am working at it," replied the sculptor.

"No later than yesterday I read in a medical journal a most interesting article on the *pigmentum* of the black races; and I bought this morning, at a book-stall on the Quai Voltaire kept by a friend of mine, a treatise on the geological formation of the Antilles."

"And what for?" asked Sainte-Lucie absolutely at a loss, although he knew the man he was dealing with.

"If I wish to execute my idea for the monument," said Labanne in a disdainful tone, "I must, before I even touch the clay, have read fifteen hundred volumes. All is contained in all. It is an artificial and wrong method to attempt to treat any subject in an isolated fashion. Hullo! you here, Godet! By what chance? I didn't see you before."

The mulatto from Bourbon Island, who was leaning against the mantelpiece, his right hand stuck between the buttons of his frock-coat, smiled bitterly.

The sculptor, having re-lighted his pipe, went on :

"I am not merely a natural force, a brute force. I am not like the bird who laid *that* monkey," pointing with the stem of his pipe to the genius of Black Liberty. "I am an intelligence, a conscience; I put thought into my work."

L

Monsieur Alidor Sainte-Lucie nodded his head approvingly; but he insisted on the sculptor giving him a drawing, a simple sketch, which he could show to the Commissioners. He was leaving for Haïti in a week.

Labanne flung himself on the sofa and seemed lost in profound meditation.

At last, after knocking the ashes from his pipe and spitting on the carpet, he looked up at the ceiling and said:

"What right have we to create imaginary beings? Phidias, or Michael-Angelo, or So-and-So makes a figure which has a semblance of life, which forces itself on our attention and penetrates to our imaginations. It is the Athene of the Parthenon, it is Moses, or the Nymph of Asnières. It is spoken about, it is dreamed about. There is a being the more in the world! What will it do then? It will perturb minds, corrupt hearts, inflame the senses, and make a fool of the public generally. Every work of art, every creation of human genius is a dangerous illusion and a guilty fraud. Sculptors, painters, and poets are magnificent liars, sublime scoundrels—nothing more. I who now speak to you, I was madly in love for six months with the Antiope of the Salon Carré, which means that for six months that rascal of a Correggio had the laugh of me.

"Do you know my friend Branchut the moralist? He is ugly, but he doesn't know it. He is poor and full of talent. His knowledge of Greek is the astonishment of all the cafés of the Quartier, and he has read Hegel. He lives on a roll of bread and a drink from the street fountains. When he has finished his bird-like repast, he writes divine things in the public gardens, or under doorways if it is raining. When he remembers, he comes and sleeps in my studio. One night he wrote a most subtle and learned commentary on the Phædo on the wall. Such is Branchut.

"Last year I lent him a coat and took him to see a Russian princess whose bust I was going to do; but she wanted the bust in marble and I could only see it in bronze. One can but realise what one sees, so the bust was never done. She was looking for a professor of literature for her daughter Fédora, an extremely beautiful girl. I proposed Branchut, and he was accepted. Thanks to my recommendation and his shabby appearance, he was paid a month in advance. He bought two shirts, took a furnished room, and made acquaintance with German sausage.

"At the sixth lesson, while he was explaining the mechanism of Homer's epic, he pinched Mademoiselle Fédora's waist so furiously that she fled uttering shrill cries. He waited, ready to make reparation for his misdeed—he would have married his noble pupil, if necessary; but he was flung out of the door. I found him in my studio that evening. 'Alas!' he said, 'it is all the fault of Saint Preux. Oh, Julie! oh, Jean-Jacques!' So you see Rousseau wrote his magnificent and passionate novel and created his:

"'Julie, amante faible et tombée avec gloire,'

just to lead my poor friend Branchut the moralist to make a fool of himself."

Monsieur Alidor Sainte-Lucie suppressed a yawn. His son, his head resting on his two hands, listened as though he were at the theatre. Monsieur Godet-Laterrasse, with a burning eye and a heaving chest, was preparing a crushing rejoinder; but Labanne rose, went to a side-table and picked up a newspaper. While he was tearing off a bit to light his pipe, his eye followed the printed lines with the instinct of the born reader.

"I say, Sainte-Lucie," he asked, "is it possible that you believe in democracy?"

At these words Godet-Laterrasse drew himself together with a little, dry, cracking noise, like that of a pistol being loaded. But the former Minister only replied by an enigmatical smile.

Labanne stated his opinions. He liked aristocracies; he would have them strong, extravagant, violent. Art only flourished under an aristocracy, he said. He regretted the cruel, elegant morals of a military nobility.

"What a mean epoch we live in!" he said. "In depriving politics of their two necessary attributes—poison and the dagger—you have made them innocent, stupid, dull, chattering and bourgeois. Society is dying for want of a Borgia. In a democracy you will have neither impressive statues, nor marble palaces, nor eloquent and great-hearted courtesans, nor chiselled sonnets, nor concerts in gardens, nor golden goblets, nor exquisite crimes, nor perils, nor adventures. You will be happy in a flat, foolish, and deadly way. So be it."

For some minutes Godet-Laterrasse had been making jerky movements, like a man who restrains himself with difficulty.

"Marvellous! marvellous!" he cried. "You are brilliantly witty, Monsieur Labanne; but remember, there are certain pleasantries which are blasphemous."

He took his hat, shook his pupil's hand, and told Monsieur Alidor he wished to say a few words to him in the hall.

Labanne heard the chinking of money, and when Monsieur Alidor re-appeared:

"What an innocent creature!" said Labanne; "but there is no harm in him."

"Hush," said Sainte-Lucie, and whispered something in Labanne's ear.

"I wish I had known you wanted a tutor. I would have sent you my friend Branchut the moralist. Well, I am going back to the Quartier. Good-bye."

This was how he spoke of what was to him the Quartier *par excellence*—the Quartier Latin.

Sainte-Lucie begged the sculptor to tell Remi, who did not know Paris, of a decent hotel near the Luxembourg.

Labanne, stroking his flaming beard, and Remi moving with the supple swing characteristic of his race, were descending the gilded staircase of the hotel side by side, when Sainte-Lucie, leaning over the banister, called out to his son :

"I warn you at once, in case I should forget, that I shall most probably not go to see General Télémaque ; but I should be glad if you would pay him a visit, and it would please your mother. He lives at Courbevoie, near the barracks. Good-bye, good-bye."

CHAPTER III

REMI could only recall vaguely the house where he was born at Port-au-Prince—the lordly mansion, in the Louis XVI. style, full of mutilated statues and half-effaced emblems; the dilapidated, crumbling inner court, planted with banana-trees; the heavy mahogany arm-chairs, ornamented with sphinxes' heads, in which he slept in the shade in the heavy noon-day silence; the luminous gaudy town, amusing as a big bazaar; and his godmother, Olivette's shop. How often, hidden behind the big cases, he had stolen the negress's bananas and sapotillas.

He could remember his mother; her burning eyes, imperious nose, greedy mouth and magnificent bronze chest, showing through a white muslin corsage, had imprinted their image on the child's memory. How often he had seen her, saturated with strong scents, her head flung back and her eyes flooded with tears, exasperating Monsieur Alidor by her brief and disdainful replies. One day he had thrown himself on her, grinding his teeth with fury, and had brought his stick down on the most beautiful shoulders in the Antilles.

But Remi had seen many things besides these. He had seen the bombardment and burning of Port-au-Prince, the pillaging, the massacres, the executions, and then more massacres and more executions. He had seen his godmother, Olivette, lying murdered in the midst of her staved-in barrels, and her assassins dead drunk with her whisky.

It was about this time that they made a long sea voyage, and landed one evening in a splendidly lighted city. France pleased him from the first. He was sent to a school in the Rue du Château at Nantes, on the benches of which he dragged out a monotonous and dreary existence, never ceasing to shiver. During the long lesson hours, he sucked sweets and drew caricatures. Every Thursday and every Sunday throughout the year the pupils, two and two in a long file, went for a walk under the old elms on the fortifications by the side of the fair, wide Loire.

He hated these promenades in the wind and the rain. He would pretend to be ill to be dispensed from them, and to be admitted to the infirmary, where he could huddle under the blankets, like a boa-constrictor in a glass case.

But he had muscles of steel when it came to

jumping over the schoolhouse wall, and running to the other end of the town to buy a bottle of rum to make punch with, in the dormitory at night. He took his studies very easily, drew the portraits of all his masters in his copybooks, passed into the rhetoric class, learnt nothing, forgot everything, was sent to Paris and confided to the care of Godet-Laterrasse.

Monsieur Sainte-Lucie had been at sea for three weeks, and the tutor had already begun the exercise of his functions by promenading his pupil on the outside of omnibuses from the Boulevard Saint-Michel to the Buttes Montmartre, and from the Madeleine to the Bastille.

Then he disappeared for a week. Remi, advised by Labanne, was living up under the tiles in a very good hotel in the Rue des Feuillantines ; he got up at noon, went out to breakfast, walked about in the sunshine, contemplating with something of a savage's delight the imitation jewellery and other attractive rubbish in the shop windows, till at five o'clock it was time to sip his sweetened vermouth. Not having heard of his tutor for eight days, he had almost forgotten him, when, on the morning of the ninth, he received a telegram, making an appointment to meet him at two o'clock on the Pont des Saints Pères.

It was freezing, and a biting wind was blowing

over the Seine. Remi took shelter, side by side with a policeman, against the cast-iron pedestal of one of the four plaster figures adorning the bridge; he stood with his shoulders hunched, and every now and then, to relieve the monotony of waiting, would stretch out his neck and watch a cargo of bullocks' horns being unloaded on the Pont Saint Nicolas. He had been there half-an-hour, and had just decided to make for the nearest café, when Monsieur Godet-Laterrasse emerged from the Louvre gateway, carrying a portfolio under his arm.

"I asked you to meet me to-day," he said, "so that we might buy the most necessary books. I am not going to bother about Virgil and Cicero; if you should need them you can find them easily enough at any of the second-hand stalls in the Rue Cujas. I am only going to see about the important ones, which will form your conscience as a man and as a citizen."

By-and-by they came to the Quai Voltaire, where they went into a bookseller's.

"Have you the works of Proudhon, Quinet, Cabet, and Esquiros?" asked Godet-Laterrasse.

The bookseller had these works, and he made a packet of them under the eyes of the buyers—a packet which Remi saw, with stupefaction, mount up like a tower.

"Sir," he said, simply, to the shopman, just as

he was tying the string, " please add to the packet two or three novels by Paul de Kock. I began one at Nantes which amused me very much, but my class-master took it from me."

The bookseller replied in a dignified tone that he did not "keep" novels, and he was beginning again to tie the string when Godet-Laterrasse stopped him. He had been thinking, and the result of his reflection was, that he borrowed from his pupil the two first volumes of Michelet's "History of France "; he wanted to look up something, he said.

They shook hands outside, and Laterrasse called out, as he scrambled on to his omnibus :

" Dig into Quinet this evening—hard."

For a moment his black silhouette stood out clearly on the top of the 'bus, then it sank, and was lost among the outlines of the ordinary people seated on the double row of benches.

When evening came, Remi was but little disposed to return to his room, where the fundamental books awaited him. He took the way to the Boulevard Saint-Michel instead, and walked towards Bullier's.

On reaching the Moorish door of the public ball-room, under which a crowd of students, shopmen, and girls were pouring in through a semicircle of gaping workmen and women, he caught sight of Labanne's golden beard. The sculptor was standing on the opposite pavement by a lamp-post, and in spite of the frost which powdered the trees, and the wind whipping the gas flame, he was reading a newspaper.

Sainte-Lucie went up to him.

"Excuse me for interrupting you," he said. "What you are reading must be very interesting."

"Not at all," replied Labanne, putting the paper in his pocket. "I was reading mechanically something very stupid. Will you come with me to 'The Famished Cat'?"

They stopped at the narrowest, the greasiest, the blackest, the smokiest, and the nastiest part of the Rue Saint-Jacques, and went into a shop full of little tables, at the end of which was a glass partition hung with white curtains. There were paintings on the walls, on the partition, on the ceiling even. For the most part they were bold, violent sketches, whose brilliant colour under the flickering of the two gas-jets was dazzling, in spite of the thick smoky atmosphere. Sainte-Lucie, who was very fond of pictures, at once singled out the most arresting canvases—a raven in the snow, and the nude body of an old woman hanging head down; a raw sirloin of beef wrapped in a piece of paper; and above all, a gutter-cat on a roof among the chimney-pots, outlining against an enormous ruddy moon its lean black back arched like a mediæval bridge. This work, by a young master of the impressionist school, served as a sign for the establishment. Several young fellows were smoking and drinking round the tables.

A fat little woman with carefully dressed hair, the bib of whose white apron swelled like a sail, looked at Labanne with tender vivacity. Grains of gunpowder seemed to sparkle in her eyes. She asked the sculptor for the terra-cotta cat he had promised her to put in the window between the dishes of sauer-kraut and salad bowls of stewed prunes.

" I have not forgotten your tabby—oh, full-handed Virginie," replied Labanne ; " but I don't see him lean enough and famished enough as yet. Furthermore, I have only read five or six volumes on cats."

Virginie, who was content to wait, told Labanne that it was most amiable of him to bring a new friend, that Monsieur Mercier and Monsieur Dion were already there, and then disappeared behind the partition—to the immediate neighbourhood of a water-tap, no doubt, for she could be heard rinsing glasses.

The new-comers sat down at a table, at which were already seated two guests, to whom Sainte-Lucie was presented. The creole soon learnt that Dion, very young, thin, and fair, was a lyric poet, and that Mercier, small and dark, with glasses on his nose, was something very vague and very important. It was hot in the tavern, and Sainte-Lucie, feeling quite at his ease, smiled so that his big mouth gaped ; while Virginie, observing him closely through the partition, concluded that he was handsome and distinguished looking. She admired his smooth, clear cheeks, so like the metal of the saucepans she polished.

The poet Dion asked Labanne, in a voice at once gentle and bitter, what had become of Bishop Gozlin.

For some time past there had been much talk at "The Famished Cat" about a statue of Bishop Gozlin, the order for which had been given, it was said, to Labanne, and which was destined to fill one of the niches of the new town-hall ; this Labanne admitted, but produced no proof. He said he could not see Bishop Gozlin standing up in a niche ; he could only see him seated in his episcopal chair.

Sainte-Lucie drank a glass of beer.

"You know," said young Dion, "that we are starting a Review. Mercier has promised me an article ; haven't you, Mercier ? You, Labanne, will do the fine arts. Monsieur Sainte-Lucie, I hope you will also give us something. We look to you to deal with the colonial question."

Sainte-Lucie had seen so much that nothing could surprise him. He was drinking—he was warm—he was happy. "I am very sorry not to be able to render you such a slight service," he replied, " but

I have just come from Nantes, where I was at
school, and I don't know anything about the
colonial question. Besides, I am not a writer."

Dion was stupefied. He could not understand
any one not being a writer; but he remembered
that creoles are rather strange people.

"Well," he said, "I shall publish my 'Wild
Love' in the first number. You know my
'Wild Love'?

> "Very old and bowed down, worn by ancient despair,
> I would wander for aye in the night of thy hair." [1]

"Did you write that?" cried Sainte-Lucie with
sincere enthusiasm. "Why, it is beautiful."

And he emptied his glass; he was delighted.

"Have you any funds for your Review?" asked
the sceptic Labanne.

"Certainly," replied the poet. "My grandmother has given me three hundred francs."

Labanne was reduced to silence. He turned over
the pages of some pamphlets he had bought on
the Quais that afternoon.

"This is a very curious volume," he said, looking
at a little book with red edges. "It is a treatise by
Saumaise (*Salmasius*) on usury (*de usuris*). I shall
give it to Branchut."

---

[1] "Très vieux, ployé, fletri par d'anciennes détresses,
Je veux errer sans fin dans la nuit de tes tresses."

Then they recollected that Branchut had not come to " The Famished Cat " that evening.

" How is poor old Branchut-du-Tic ? " asked the poet Dion.   " Is he still falling at the feet of Russian princesses ? He must give us an article for the Review."

Sainte-Lucie asked Labanne if this Monsieur Branchut-du-Tic was the professor of literature he had heard him speak of one day at the Grand Hotel."

" The same, young man," said Labanne.   " You will see him.   But I must tell you that his name is simply Claude Branchut.   His nose, which is very long, is agitated by nervous shivers, and afflicted with a strange undulating movement ; hence the nickname we have bestowed on him.   For the matter of that, Cato of Utica (*Caton d'Utique*) and Branchut-du-Tic are both Stoics."

" Monsieur Sainte-Lucie," said the poet, " I will read my verses to you, so that you can make your criticisms before they are published."

" No, no," cried Mercier, his little round face contracting under his spectacles ; " you can read your verses to him when you are alone."

Then the conversation turned on æsthetics. Dion considered that poetry was the natural and primeval language.

Mercier replied sourly.

" It was cries, not verses, which were the primitive and natural language. The first men did not exclaim:

"Yea, to his temple I come the Eternal to worship."

They said, "*hoo hoo hoo! ba ba ba! quack!*" But are you a mathematician? No? Then it is no use arguing with you. I only argue with an adversary who knows the mathematical method."

Labanne asserted that poetry was a sublime monstrosity, a magnificent disease. For him, a fine poem was a fine crime, and nothing else.

"Allow me," said Mercier, adjusting his spectacles. "How far have you gone in mathematical analysis? I shall know by your answers if I can argue with you or not."

Sainte-Lucie, emptying a fresh glass, said to himself: "My new friends are very peculiar, but very agreeable."

Finally, as he understood literally nothing of the discussion, which became heated, he gave up trying to follow the tangled thread of discourse, and let his naïf bold eyes wander round the room. They encountered the amorous eyes of the fat Virginie, who, leaning against the glass door of the partition, was watching him as she wiped her red hands.

"She is a very agreeable woman," he thought. Having drunk another *bock*, he became more confirmed in this opinion.

M

The tavern had emptied little by little. The founders of the Review alone remained round the saucers piled up on the table, like two porcelain towers in a Chinese village.

Virginie was about to pull down the iron shutters in front, when the door opened and a long pale person came in, dressed in a very short summer-jacket, with the collar turned up. Two enormous, flat, and abominably shod feet protruded in front of him.

"It is Branchut," cried the Committee. "How do you do, Branchut?"

But Branchut was in a sombre mood.

"Labanne," he said, "you took away, by mistake I sincerely hope, the key of your studio, and if I had not met you here, I should inevitably have had to pass the night out of doors."

Branchut spoke with Ciceronian elegance. His eyes rolled terribly, and his nose twitched nervously from the root to the nostrils, but his mouth emitted only the purest and most dulcet sounds.

Labanne handed over his key, with an apology. Branchut would drink neither beer, coffee, cognac, nor chartreuse. He would not drink anything. Dion asked him for an article for his Review, but the moralist required a deal of coaxing.

"Take his commentary on the Phædo," said Labanne, "which is written in charcoal all along the wall of my studio. You can have it copied, unless you prefer to take the wall to the printer."

As soon as they left off asking him, he promised to write something. "It shall be," he said, "a study in a particular style on the philosophers."

He coughed, an oratorical cough, picked up an empty glass, placed it in front of him and proceeded leisurely.

"This is my point of view. There are two sorts of philosophers: those who place themselves behind the glass, like Hegel, and those who place themselves between the glass and myself, like Kant. Do you understand the point of view?"

Dion understood the point of view, so Branchut was able to continue.

"When," he said, "a philosopher is behind my glass, do you know what I do——?"

Here, having put out one of the lights and turned down the other, Virginie warned the gentlemen that it was half-past twelve, and they must go. Branchut, Mercier, and Labanne went out one after the other, stooping under the half-lowered shutter.

Sainte-Lucie, left alone in the dark shop, seized Virginie round the waist and gave her three or four kisses, wherever he could snatch them, on her neck or on her ear. Virginie resisted a moment, then she burst into sobs, and melted into the mulatto's arms.

Branchut, meanwhile, standing on the pavement, was saying to Labanne: "Do you think I would take my glass and put it behind the philosopher? No! Or take the philosopher and—— ?"

"Aren't you coming, Sainte-Lucie?" cried the poet Dion, who was counting on reciting his verses to the creole all the way home.

But Sainte-Lucie did not answer.

CHAPTER IV

T was snowing that morning; the muffled sound of the passing carriages came heavily through the windows of "The Famished Cat." A livid light threw up the pictures on the wall harshly, and made the painted figures look like corpses. Remi was seated at a little table in the deserted shop, devouring a beefsteak and potatoes, while Virginie stood motionless in front of him, her hands folded on her apron, her eyes contemplating him with the expression of a saint.

"It is tender, isn't it?" she said effusively. "Have you enough? There is a fine cut of cold roast beef in the kitchen; will you have some? You don't drink anything."

He was eating and drinking as hard as he could, while she eyed him devoutly. She said:

"I have given you some Gruyère cheese, which is so good it is *creeping*. Monsieur Potrel was very fond of Gruyère, especially when it crept.".

Remi went on eating.

Then Virginie gave him fruit and jam in addition.

She remained absorbed for a long time in her mystic meditation, then sighed and said:

"Perhaps I am wrong in doing as I do. You will be like all the others, Monsieur Sainte-Lucie. All men are alike. But I am not like the average woman. When I attach myself to some one it is for life. I have told you how Potrel behaved to me. Now, frankly, was that the way to act? A man for whom I did everything. I mended his linen; I would have gone to the stake for him. He was clever, talented, everything, but he was ungrateful."

And the afflicted eyes of the lady turned to the picture of "The Famished Cat," as though to bid it bear witness to the ingratitude of Potrel.

Her ample chest heaved, her three chins trembled, as she added in a stifled voice:

"And to think that I am not sure that I don't still love him! If you were to abandon me I don't know what I should do. Are you coming this evening, darling?—What can I offer you, gentlemen?"

This last phrase, accompanied by a smile, was addressed to two customers who came in just then.

Sainte-Lucie was happy; he had been plucked gloriously by the examiners, but he warmed himself at every friendly stove, laughed his big sensual laugh, and amused himself with everything he saw and heard, without troubling about anything further. The very slightly dissimulated favour with which Virginie regarded him had won him the respect of the guests at " The Famished Cat." Women mark with a distinctive sign the men they favour.

He found Labanne's studio even more attractive than Virginie's room. But the stove was never lighted. This made Remi angry; he was already a good draughtsman, and was beginning to paint. Labanne said :

"That fellow draws by instinct. He has no ideas, but he has the touch. I really believe that one must be as stupid as Potrel to model as well as he does."

Godet-Laterrasse had tried several times to recapture his pupil. He would come down sometimes towards mid-day, outside an omnibus from the heights of Montmartre, would burst breathlessly into Remi's room and cry out :

"Dig into Tacitus. Cheer up !"

He would say emphatically : *Nox eadem Britannici necem atque rogum conjunxit.*[1] Then he would get muddled over certain grammatical difficulties from which he would extricate himself by wandering remarks about the great writer, who, he said, had branded the foreheads of tyrants with a red-hot iron.

---

[1] A single night witnessed the death and the obsequies of Britannicus.

The lesson over, he would get up, and with a lordly gesture lay hold of two or three volumes of Prudhon or Quinet, which slumbered unopened on the chest of drawers, and saying that he wished to refer to them, would put them under his arm. Remi never saw them again. In a few months' time there was nothing but a few odd books left of the enormous packet, and these he took one day and sold to a bookseller in the Rue Soufflot. There was no longer any talk about the fundamental works.

CHAPTER V

IME went by. Monsieur Godet-Laterrasse came now and then, to give his pupil a lesson. "The Famished Cat" did not occupy all of Remi's mind; he would stay in his room, munching exotic dainties, which he bought at the creole grocery in the Rue Tronchet.

Every day, now the weather was fine, he would open his window and look out into the street. He liked to see the horses go by; they seemed to him thin in the collar, long in the body, and big in the crupper. Of the women who passed below across the front of the hotel, he could only see the tops of their hats, their hair, their skirts puffed out behind, and occasionally a chin and a bust under it. He noticed the graceful swing or the comical waddle of all these creatures, going on their easy or difficult way. Such fugitive aspects of life amused him, and he did not spoil the spectacle by reflection. For no deep thought had as yet germinated under his thick hair.

What interested him most was the house opposite,

which reared in front of his hotel its façade of new stone, with five windows to each storey. Through the half-open windows he could see bits of the wall papers, the woodwork of the dining-room, ends of gilded picture frames, and corners of furniture. All these things, diminished by distance (for the street was wide), appeared to him of the size and importance of a toy. The people who moved about in the rooms looked like marvellously finished dolls. If some startled head suddenly popped up among the tiles, through a skylight, and showed in the sunshine a bald cranium or a pair of winking eyes, the creole would go off in a long fit of laughter, and be inspired with dozens of sketches, which he afterwards tore up. In a few days he was familiar with all the people who moved about in the great stone hive across the way.

On the balcony of the fifth floor a half-pay captain (such he most surely was) sowed flower seeds in a box. On the intermediate storeys servants were to be seen beating fur rugs at the windows. Sometimes Remi would see a broom moving in front of the furniture, somnolent under its shroud-like coverings against the white panels. On the ground floor a house agent's clerk stood at a high desk and wrote throughout the day.

But Remi's eyes turned most frequently to the rooms on the fourth floor. There was never any-

thing strange or mysterious there, nothing voluptuous, nothing which could call the blood to the
young man's cheeks. The only remarkable thing
about the windows was a cage full of canaries and
a very small pot of flowers. The apartment lighted
by these windows was occupied by a middle-aged
lady, slow but active and calm in her movements :
her placid face, which appeared first at one window
and then at another, was crowned by beautiful hair,
which was nevertheless getting a little wide in the
parting. Her daughter, who was still a child in
short frocks, had inherited her mother's hair, but it
was fairer and more luminous in quality, abundant
and rich ; she wore it separated in two masses by a
fine line. She moved about like a boy, and did not
know what to do with her arms and legs.

Remi entered, unseen, into the intimacy of these
two people ; he knew all the little monotonous
events of their existence, the time for meals and for
lessons, the time to go for a walk, and to bring in
the bird-cage, the time when, armed with notepaper and books, to go off to classes. He knew
that the ladies went out at eleven o'clock every
Sunday, with prayer-books in their hands. At ten
o'clock every morning during the week, the young
girl sat down to the piano, whose brass handle
shone near the window in the gilded drawing-room.
Remi could see two little red hands, child's hands,

running up and down the notes, playing scales he
could not hear.

But she did not stay very long seated on the
music-stool before the piano. She came to the
window, and, if it was shut, lifted up the white
curtain and looked into the street with frank
audacity, and pressed the end of a small nose
against the glass so that it became flat and white:
then she would disappear as she had come, as a bird
takes flight, without any appreciable reason. Both
mother and daughter had large limpid eyes, childish
eyes, emotionless eyes, which seemed to say,
"Nothing has ever troubled, or ever will trouble,
our affectionate peacefulness." The mother, who
had no doubt been a widow for many years, was
the quieter of the two. The kindly nature of the
plump woman was visible in all her gestures, affectionate without being caressing, vigilant without
being tiresome. Mademoiselle was more *brusque*.
One day she even opened the window and leaned
out on the balcony and made signs to two of her
companions at church or school who were passing in
the street below.

She did not show the slightest confusion when
her mother fetched her in, and sent the maid, as
Remi supposed, to ask the young ladies upstairs:
they came up and evidently had very funny things
to say to each other, for all three laughed merrily.

And their laughter reached Remi's ears, across the wide roadway, like the scarcely perceptible sound of scattering pearls.

Every day Remi walked by the Luxembourg Gardens, through the railings in the light morning mist he could see the undulating lawns and the groups of exotic plants. He would go on to the Rue Carnot and into the studio, the key of which was always left for him under the mat.

Labanne's studio was so full of books that it might have been taken for a second-hand shop. Books were piled round abandoned studies, shrinking under their dry cloths. The floor was entirely covered with piled up books. One walked over leather bindings. Calf-skin backs, with gilded lines and corners, red edges, speckled edges, yellow, blue and red backs, many of them half torn off, lay about in heaps. Big dog-eared folios yawned in every corner, and the boards dropped to pieces beneath the shrivelling leather. A thick layer of dust slowly buried this mass of literature and science.

The walls had once been whitewashed. Bare, so far as the upper half was concerned, they were scribbled over to the height of a man's head, in small text hand, half in Greek half in French. It was the commentary on the Phædo, which Branchut had been inspired to write one sleepless night. The door was covered with inscriptions, traced by various people.

The topmost one, cut with a knife in capital letters, said:

> "Woman is more bitter than death."

The second, in round hand, in crayon, ran:

> "Academicians are all bourgeois, Cabanel is a hairdresser's assistant."

The third in pencil, in a cursive hand, said:

> "Laud we the womanly form, which still, as of old, uplifts
> Chants hieratic, in praise of the greatest of beauty's gifts." [1]
> PAUL DION.

The fourth, written in chalk, in an illiterate hand, said:

> "I have brought back the clean linen. Monday I will call for the dirty at the porter's lodge."

The fifth in charcoal, by Labanne himself, said:

> "Athens, ever venerable city, if thou hadst not existed, the world would not yet know the meaning of beauty."

The sixth, inscribed with a hair-pin, which had faintly scratched the paint, declared:

> "Labanne is a rat. I don't care a damn for him.—MARIA."

And there were many others on the door.

In a corner near the stove a horse-blanket was

---

[1] "Gloire aux corps féminins qui, sur le mode antique,
Chantent l'hymne sacré de la beauté plastique."

flung on a pile of books and papers. These papers, these books, and this horse-blanket formed the bed of the moralist Branchut.

One day when he was sitting on his horse-blanket dreaming about Demosthenes, German professors, and the Princess Fédora, Remi was copying a watering-pot and putting his tongue out in the excess of his preoccupation. Wanting to change a line in his drawing, he asked the philosopher if he had any stale bread-crumb in his pocket, and inadvertently addressed him as Monsieur Branchut-du-Tic. Branchut, whom misfortune had made irascible, looked at him with eyes goggling like a lobster, a formidable shiver ran down his nose, and he left the studio in a rage.

The poet Dion, whom he found at the tavern, and Labanne, whom he discovered in front of a box of old books on the quay, took the matter in hand. The poet Dion declared that blood alone could wipe out the insult, but the sceptic Labanne was more humane, and brought about a sort of reconciliation. Remi bore no malice.

The moralist and the creole lived in peace for a month or two; till Branchut, whose fate it was to suffer through women, had the misfortune to look tenderly at the hostess of " The Famished Cat." Now Branchut's face, when he wished to express tenderness, was terribly like the face of an epileptic.

He ogled Virginie with bloodshot eyes starting
from their orbits; she was terrified, and made a
great fuss about her fright. She took every occasion to show the philosopher that he inspired
her with virtuous horror; and as at the same
time she cast languishing looks at Remi, Branchut suffered all the pangs of jealousy. He was
unhappy, and became spiteful.

First of all he found fault with the gentle
Labanne, who had doubly wronged him, inasmuch
as he was possessed of a small private income, and
had rendered the philosopher many services.

Solemnly every morning Branchut would return
him the key of the studio, and every morning
the sculptor quietly put it under the mat, where
every evening Branchut would come and find it.

During the months of July and August Branchut
became bitter, sceptical, and strong-minded. He
posed as the superior man. He despised women,
and said they were inferior beings. He affected
not to look at Virginie, when he haughtily demanded bottles of beer from her, for which
Labanne paid.

He put forth transcendental theories on art.

"I saw recently in a museum," he said, "the
figure of a mammoth traced with a bit of pointed
flint on a piece of fossil ivory. This figure dates
from a prehistoric period—it predates the oldest

of civilisations. It is the work of a stupid savage. But it reveals an artistic sentiment far superior to the most beautiful conceptions of Michael Angelo: it is at once ideal and true. And our best modern artists sacrifice truth to the ideal, or the ideal to truth."

Here he looked maliciously at Labanne, but the latter was quite happy; he approved and even enlarged on his philosopher friend's idea.

" Art," he said, " declines in proportion as thought develops. There were no sculptors left in Greece at the time of Aristotle. Artists are inferior creatures; they are like pregnant women—they bring forth they know not how. Praxiteles produced his Venus as the mother of Aspasia produced Aspasia—quite naturally and quite foolishly. The sculptors of Athens and Rome had not read the Abbé Winckelmann. They knew nothing of æsthetics, yet they made the Theseus of the Parthenon and the Augustus of the Louvre. A clever man produces nothing beautiful or great."

Branchut asked sourly:

" Then in that case why are you a sculptor—you who think you are a clever man? It is true that I have never seen anything of yours which resembled the least bit in the world a statue, a bust, or a bas-relief. You haven't even a clay model or a sketch to show, and it is certainly five years since you

N

touched a chisel. If you keep your studio simply
as a refuge for me, I owe it to you and I owe it to
myself to tell you that I should not have the
slightest trouble in finding another lodging. I have
not given you, that I know of, the right to crush
me with your charity."

But in spite of the greatness of his soul the philosopher could not remain long on these heights ;
he became weak once more. He forgot the
mammoth in the museum, and could see none but
Virginie. He fell into a deadly depression ; yet he
had a brief, bright hour in his life. He met
Virginie one morning coming back from market,
a basket on each arm, sweating, puffing, coughing,
and choking with incipient asthma. He followed
her, rather reluctantly, and she allowed him to carry
the basket of meat. He was delighted, but his joy
was the cause of his downfall. He hoped and dared
everything. One evening he slipped into the kitchen
and seized her in his arms as she was washing the
dishes. She dropped a plate and emitted heart-
rending cries ; the Princess Fédora did not shriek
so shrilly. This raised a great scandal. The poet
Dion was pleased ; Mercier's eyes twinkled behind
his glasses ; Labanne shrugged his shoulders. Remi
was a little vexed, but he smiled to himself when
he hit on a scheme for revenge.

It was the vengeance of a schoolboy and a

savage, and he licked his lips at the thought of it. He let it sleep in his greedy lazy heart, like a pot of jam in a good housekeeper's store-closet.

The poet Dion was again talking about starting a review. The attempt of the previous year had failed because his grandmother's three hundred francs had to be wasted in domestic expenses; but he had received another present of the same sum.

"We must find a title," he said.

For two hours they discussed any number of possible and impossible appellations.

The next day Dion saluted the assembly at "The Famished Cat" with a triumphant cry:

"I've got it: *The Idea. The Idea: A new Review.*"

And with his head on one side, his Apollo-like locks thrown back, his face illuminated by a smile, he turned over the pages of an imaginary magazine and read out, as it were in capital letters: "*The Idea: A new Review.* Paul Dion, editor."

"What idea?" asked Labanne, stroking his yellow beard.

"The idea of the mathematical basis, of course," replied Mercier.

"The idea of the superiority of poetry and ideality over prose and reality," replied Dion.

"And also, perhaps," insinuated the moralist Branchut in bitter-sweet tones, rubbing his flexible nose, "and also, perhaps, the idea of the new morality of which I propose to expound the theory, that is of course if it is agreeable to you."

Labanne remarked that the thing had better be called *The Ideas*, and not *The Idea*, as each one seemed to have his own.

But the first title was adhered to, and Dion wrote out on a sheet of notepaper, with the pen Virginie used for her accounts, a summary of the first number, which was to contain:

1. "An Address to the Reader," by Paul Dion.

2. "An article, as yet vague, on philosophy," by Claude Branchut.

3. "An article, still more vague, on the fine arts," by Émile Labanne.

4. "The Mistress who brings Death—a Poem," by Paul Dion.

5. "Something very vague on science," by Guillaume Mercier.

As to theatrical and literary criticisms, the editor would look after them.

The matter thus decided on, Dion discovered, in a badly-paved street near Saint-André des Arts, a printer in distress, who with dull indifference consented to print the magazine. He was a little, pale, bald man, whose melting-away aspect made one think of a candle-end burning in a draught. His affairs were in a pitiful condition. He was a

hopeless printer, but he was a printer. He printed.
He sent proofs which Dion befouled on all the
tables in the café. But they were obliged to admit
that copy was lacking, in spite of sundry poems
sent from divers parts of Europe to the editor
in chief of *The Idea.*

The first number seemed likely to be the more
slender, since Branchut lost the pages of his article
on philosophy in the various doorways as fast as he
wrote them, and Labanne could not compose the
first lines of his studies on art until he had read
fifteen hundred volumes. Mercier's article did
really exist; but the author, who was as cramped
in his writing, in his style, and in his ideas, as he
was in his clothes, could easily have put the whole
thing on the two glasses of his spectacles. As
for "The Mistress who brings Death," she was
already in her third proof.

It was at this moment that Sainte-Lucie, appointed
Secretary to the Staff, proposed to introduce Monsieur Godet-Laterrasse to the poet; he could not
help but give them an article, he said.

It was a great occasion the night on which Godet-
Laterrasse climbed down from the outside of an
omnibus and entered Virginie's establishment. He
turned the door-handle with the air of a man who
knows himself in demand, and while his entrance
was received with a flattering murmur, he crossed

the shop with African majesty, tempered by creole languor. When he heard himself hailed as "dear master" by the poet Dion, he showed every tooth in his head, and smiled like an idol. But all of a sudden his face assumed an expression of haughty dislike. He had met Labanne's indifferent glance through the tobacco smoke. He had heard that Labanne had declared that he was going to represent him in an heroic attitude, with the dial of a clock in his waistcoat. Since then he considered him to be the most corrupt of sceptics. Filled with this thought, he turned his horizontal face towards Dion and Mercier, and said:

"Young men, beware of scepticism; it is a poisonous breath which dries up the soul in its flower."

He promised to contribute to the magazine an unpublished chapter of his great work on the regeneration of humanity by the black races.

He explained his theory. The black races were untouched by the Christian leprosy, which for eighteen centuries had devoured the white peoples.

He told how, when he was but eleven years old, he was walking alone by the sea, and, looking at its immensity, he said to himself: "Priests can say what they like; I will never believe that Christianity has done anything for the abolition of slavery."

When he left, they escorted him to the omnibus. As it approached Sainte-Lucie hailed it. Godet-Laterrasse, having shaken hands all round, took his pupil affectionately by the shoulders, and, drawing him a little to one side, said:

"I have forgotten my purse; it is most careless of me! Lend me a few sous."

Then, having adroitly picked up a franc from the handful of change held out to him, he climbed on to the vehicle and called out:

"Go ahead, Remi! Dig into Tacitus!"

CHAPTER VI

T was quite natural that Remi should be plucked when he went up for his examination the second time. His prospects of a degree were becoming more and more misty and effaced. When Monsieur Godet-Laterrasse commented on his failures, which were certainly not surprising, he managed to make them appear mysterious and questionable.

"It is not you who have been plucked," he said ; "it is I. They were aiming at me when they hit you, you may be sure. Ah! these gentlemen of the Sorbonne won't forgive me my last article."

When Remi heard remarks of this kind, he felt so completely knocked over that he did not exactly know if the baccalaureate was a literary examination or a secret society.

He passed the winter in a voluptuous torpor, and when the timid April sun shone on the walls it only half-awakened him.

The sparrows were twittering on the roofs. The half-pay captain was sowing seeds in his green boxes.

Windows, which had been closed for so long, their panes obscured by thick steam, now opened to the pale daylight and the first warm breath of spring. Remi, who had since the summer lost sight and recollection of his friends on the fourth storey, was pleased to see the cage full of canaries and the brass handle of the piano again.

When he caught sight, for the first time, of the mother and daughter in the gilt salon, he almost bowed in a friendly way to them.

A little old man was sitting on the sofa holding his hat and his umbrella between his knees; he seemed to be talking to them in an intimate fashion. He raised his arm, and Remi imagined that he was saying :

"How you have grown, Marie (or Jeanne, or Louise)! Why, you are quite a young lady!"

Remi felt a little cross at seeing a stranger seated in this fashion on his friend's sofa—not that the little old man was unpleasant looking; on the contrary, he had the air of a good fellow. But Remi did not know him, and the thought that the ladies had secrets from him made him unhappy. One cannot foresee everything. He shut his window, and sulked till the next day. He opened it in the morning just to see if the canaries' cage was in its usual place, and saw the young girl, in a round hat, chewing the top of her

umbrella and prancing with the impatience of a
young horse—a habit of hers when she was ready
to go out, and had to wait while her mother
loitered, tying her bonnet-strings in front of the
glass. But one must admit that a woman of
forty-five can't dress as a little girl can in two or
three birdlike darts.

The mother that day, as every day, inspected her
daughter's toilet minutely. But there must have
been something seriously wrong with the grey frock,
for she said something which was received with all
sorts of little impatient pouting movements with
stamping and marks of despair. Finally, Mademoiselle undid the buttons of her corsage and
pushed-to the window, which in a few seconds
opened again of its own accord, so that Remi
caught a glimpse of the mother standing up with
the grey frock in her hand; she was putting a
stitch in it, while Mademoiselle, clad in her stays
and a short white petticoat, stood waiting.

She turned her head, and saw the student looking
at her; then, with the pretty gesture of a child
who is being bathed and is chilly, she covered her
chest with her two arms. Her lips pronounced
some words very rapidly, which were surely:

" Mamma—mamma."

The mother shrugged her shoulders, and seemed
to answer quite calmly:

"Good Lord, my dear! What does it matter?" Then she closed the window nonchalantly.

From that day Remi refrained, though he could not have said why, from observing his opposite neighbours too closely; but he thought they might go away, and he would never see them again, and the thought made him sad. He decided that the degree, as understood by Godet-Laterasse, was not a very important matter, and he resolved to be a painter. To paint seemed to him at once fine and simple. Then suddenly he remembered General Télémaque.

"I must go and see him," he said.

CHAPTER VII

FTER his second failure, Monsieur Godet-Laterrasse, who was much taken up with public affairs, neglected his pupil considerably. Remi consoled himself for the absence of his tutor by drawing in Labanne's studio. The incomparable sculptor had recently discovered the works of the poet Colardeau in a box on the parapet of the Quai Malaquais, and was carried away with admiration for them.

"Colardeau is the greatest of all French poets," he said.

A heavy heat hung over the city of stone and asphalt, but the moralist Branchut was clothed in a thick overcoat of cloth with a long pile, which, one of his friends said, made him look like a scythe covered with goat's skin. His thoughts dwelt perpetually on woman, and he had never been in such a ferocious humour. He no longer had the appetite with which he had formerly eaten a ha'penny roll every day, but an inextinguishable thirst burnt him under his thick fleece. One day when Remi, under Labanne's direction, was copying for the hundredth time the water-jar, which stood in the winter on the studio stove, the moralist Branchut seized the model vase and went off to fill it at the pump. When he returned, with a wet nose and a dripping beard, the young creole cast a sidelong glance, full of meaning, at him. Branchut called for lightning from heaven, and longed for the deluge. He wrote obscure and terrible sentiments on leaves which he tore from Labanne's most valuable books. A storm freshened the atmosphere of the city and relieved the moralist's over-strained nerves.

Time went by, the passing seasons brought kites in the windy September skies, fogs on the October horizon, hot chestnuts at the doors of the wine shops, oranges on the barrows, the magic-lantern on the Savoyard's back; and when the roofs were covered with snow, the savoury smell of roasted goose in warm dining-rooms, on feast days, such as Christmas, New Year, and Twelfth Night. But time did not change Branchut's heart.

Towards four o'clock on the afternoon of Twelfth Night, Remi was crossing the Place Saint-Sulpice with the poet Dion; he looked at the icicles which hung from the four stone bishops and half hid them, and at the frozen water in the fountain under their feet. He rubbed his hands together, and laughed aloud.

"It won't be very warm on this Place at midnight," he said.

Then they began to discuss—Remi with childish joy, and Dion with more refined satisfaction—a letter they had just sent off by a commissionaire, the opening phrases of which they repeated to one another untiringly:

"You are dark and I am fair. You are strong and I am weak. I understand you, and I love you."

They had evidently concocted some detestable practical joke, with which they felt pleased and proud.

That evening Branchut dined at "The Famished Cat" with Mercier, who was beginning to look old, and whose shrunken face was almost hidden by his spectacles, with Labanne, who had been much taken up for a week past with a seventeenth-century book on etiquette, the poet Dion, and Sainte-Lucie. Virginie gave them a cabbage soup of powerful bouquet. Branchut pushed away the smoking plateful Labanne offered him. Such heavy food choked him, he said. Labanne had not the slightest idea how to feed one of the *élite*.

A commissionaire came in, asked for Monsieur Branchut, and handed him a violet-scented letter in a pearl-grey envelope with a blue monogram. As the philosopher read it, his sensitive nose

twitched violently. At last he put it in his pocket
(he was wearing a dress-coat Labanne had given
him), and looked around mysteriously. All his
thin and acrid blood rushed to his pimpled face;
he was transfigured. His nose seemed illuminated
by an interior flame. Dion was examining the
hem of his table-napkin; Remi, with his knife in
the salt-cellar, was making hills and valleys with
the salt, and seemed entirely lost in the contemplation of the little polar landscapes he was
creating, and destroying with the all-powerful
capriciousness of a Lapland Jehovah.

The conversation which the commissionaire had
interrupted was quietly resumed, Labanne alone
talking with any energy. Much interested in the
etiquette of polite manners in the seventeenth
century, he was regretting the days of Louis XIV.,
and said:

"The Great King was certainly not to be com-
pared with Cæsar Borgia, but anyway he was better
than the rights of man and immortal principles!"

Every now and then Branchut slipped his hand
into the pocket of his coat and pressed something
to his heart. He was lost in a profound reverie,
and from his swollen and cracked lips there escaped
at intervals suave words alluding to the possible
regeneration of mankind by love. At eleven o'clock
he rose to go out; first brushing his waistcoat with

his cuff, which showed for him extraordinary re-
finement and unwonted attention to his personal
appearance.

"See you to-morrow?" asked Labanne.   The
philosopher muttered mysteriously something about
the probability of his total disappearance, and departed as quietly and swiftly as if he had wings.
Shortly after, Dion and Labanne left "The
Famished Cat."

At midnight the moralist, in his dress-coat, was
still walking round and round the fountain with its
four bishops.   The few belated passers-by went
quickly across the square.   The water which had
overflowed from the basin of the fountain froze on
the asphalt, and Branchut slipped at every step.
A bitter wind blew through the tails of his coat;
but like a blind horse turning a mill-wheel, he
turned and turned about the stone fountain inde-
fatigably.   The town-hall clock struck one and
still the moralist revolved; the silence of the night
was broken only by the monotonous tread of two
policemen on their beat.   At half-past one he drew
out the scented note and read it over by the light
of a street lamp.

"You are dark and I am fair.   You are strong
and I am weak.   I understand you, and I love you.
Come to-night at twelve o'clock to the fountain on
the Place Saint-Sulpice."

There could be no mistaking that, so the philosopher returned to his post. The hoar-frost covered him with a glittering powder; the tails of his coat hung heavy with moisture. The square was deserted. Still he waited. Deceived, disappointed, overcome, he dropped on to a bench and sat there motionless, his head in his hands. When at last he looked up, he thought he caught sight of Dion and Sainte-Lucie disappearing swiftly in the obscurity of the Rue Honoré-Chevalier. A sudden light burst in upon him; his nose trembled with indignation.

He swore to Labanne next day, as he lay draped in his horse-blanket, that he would kill Sainte-Lucie.

"I don't care much for my life," he said, "but I care still less for his."

Labanne tried in vain to pacify him.

At the same time Remi was quietly and obliviously enjoying the warmth of his eider-down quilt, thinking to himself the while:

"I really must go and see General Télémaque one of these days."

CHAPTER VIII

TÉLÉMAQUE, a linen cap on his head, a white apron round his waist, stood smiling on the threshold of his shop. The dusty avenue, with its meagre plane trees, was inundated by the bright morning sunshine. To the right the view extended as far as the barracks, from whence came a sound of trumpets; to the left, to the round, open space where the Emperor's statue should have been, but where there was only an empty pedestal. On either side of the wide avenue were low houses and bits of waste ground, with washerwomen's clothes-poles in rows. The wine shops at the street corners overlooking these bare patches were painted a brown-red, to attract the eye, and provoke the thirst of soldiers and workmen, even from a distance. All the rest, walls and waste ground alike, were a uniform grey. The two houses opposite to that occupied by Télémaque had plaster façades and were three storeys high. They were ornamented with balustrades, semi-circular bow-windows, and niches containing busts —all cracking, peeling, mouldy, their broken windows patched with paper and hung with rags. Groups of children and dogs played in confused heaps in the dust, soldiers were walking slowly towards the river-bank, and straight-petticoated women came and went, carrying pails and baskets.

Télémaque's shop was painted red; in the window were to be seen a sirloin of beef and some steaks laid out on plates. Télémaque was swinging a dead rabbit by the ears and smiling. The lustrous enamel of his eyes subdued yet at the same time set off by his plump cheeks, illuminated his ebony face, with its flat nose and thick lips. His wool was still black and curly, but his forehead, which had yielded to a rectilinear baldness, rose as it receded, disclosing a portion of the skull of which the summit formed a sort of crest.

Miragoane, sitting on her haunches, looked with equal interest at men, animals, and things. Free from disturbing passions, her mind at ease, she warmed herself quietly in the sun. Sometimes she would stretch up her intelligent head and with curled-up tongue lick a little of the coagulated blood on the muzzle of the rabbit as it hung from Télémaque's hands; then, satisfied with this delicate piece of sensuality, she would look down the avenue again, and softly stir her tail.

Télémaque turned the skin of the rabbit inside out as easily as one turns a glove, then putting the skinless animal, glowing with the most brilliant

hues, upon a small table, he adroitly cut it up
and put the pieces in a dish.   Then he went into
the shop, the outer door of which opened on to
a little garden in which were several arbours.
Having prepared his stew in the cleanest way, he
sat down and dreamily watched the copper saucepan singing on the stove.   His eyes, which were
like the freshly-painted eyes on a new doll, stared
vacantly; but no doubt they saw more than the
tiled stove, the pewter counter, and the tables
covered with American cloth, for he was murmuring to himself a strange, low chant, and talking
to invisible beings.   Then, having taken another
look at the stew, which, as the cooks say, had
started on a slow fire:

"Miragoane," he said, "keep the shop."

Miragoane turned an intelligent eye on him, and
came forward as far as the doorstep, where she sat
down with an important air.   Télémaque went upstairs to a nice bedroom hung with a pictured paper
on which a boar-hunt was indefinitely repeated.
This room was furnished with a walnut wardrobe, a
bed with white cotton hangings, and four tables, and
served as the landlord's bedroom and as a dining-
room for private parties on Sundays.   Télémaque
took a box out of the cupboard, and laying it on
the table, opened it with much care.   It was full
of things wrapped in paper and silk handkerchiefs.
He took out first a red shawl, then a pair of

beaded epaulettes, some earrings, a cross, a regular plaster of obscure orders, and a big hat trimmed with braid and big gold tassels at each of its two points. When these treasures were spread on the table, he contemplated them with the astonished look of a child; he put the hat with its dangling tassels on his woolly head, wrapped himself in the red shawl, which had belonged to his wife Olivette, and looked at himself in his small shaving mirror.

He was living his past life over again, and had gone back to the time when he was a general. He saw the dazzling coronation ceremony of His Majesty Faustin I., the blue mantles of the dukes, princes and counts, the red coats of the barons; the black face of the Emperor with his golden crown; Olivette, who had come all in her court-dress, in a wheelbarrow, to take her place with the other ladies in the nave of the church.

Everything came back to him, the multi-coloured garments, the salutes of the cannon, the military, music, the cries of " Vive l'Empereur." His imagination pictured the sumptuous entertainments of the imperial palace, where, beneath the candles and the crystal chandeliers, the ladies of the court danced, till in the furious excitement of waltzing their magnificent black bosoms burst through their white muslin bodices. He saw again his soldiers, drawn up for inspection on the arid and sunburnt plain. Ranked in order of battle they all presented arms to him, while he himself, Télémaque, with his hands behind his back, like Napoleon in the pictures, went up and down the ranks, and said:

"Soldiers, I am very pleased with you."

Then his imagination presented more sombre pictures. He saw the events which had brought about his fall.

Soulouque, the Emperor, combined with his power as a sovereign the genius of a crafty and cruel child. In December 1851 he determined to make war on the Republic of San Domingo, and General Télémaque, at the head of his brigade, formed part of the expeditionary corps commanded by General Voltaire Castor, Comte de l'Ile-à-Vache. In his proclamation to the army the Emperor said: "Officers, non-commissioned officers, soldiers! The men of the East, the cattle graziers of San Domingo, will fly before you. Forward!"

Full of confidence in his Emperor's word, General Télémaque marched proudly at the head of the black regiments which formed the vanguard—his tasselled hat on his head, and on his breast the imperial and military Order of Saint Faustin, as well as the grand cordon of the Haïtian Legion of Honour. His uniform was heavily braided with gold, but his feet were bare. All of a sudden a vigorous rattle of musketry surprised him on the border of a plantation of bananas. Astonished, indignant, frightened, he turned his troubled face to his troops, and cried with sincere eloquence :

" Emperor made fun of poor people ! "

At the general's words the brigade turned on its heels and ran off as fast as it could. Télémaque headed the flying column, putting into play the muscles of his monkey-like legs, and hanging out his tongue. He didn't give one thought to the guns, the tents, the packets of cartridges, and the cases of biscuit abandoned by the roadside. When Soulouque heard of this military achievement, he trembled in every limb. He had General Voltaire Castor shot by way of raising his spirits somewhat, and he ordered General Télémaque to be arrested; but the latter hid for a week in the bush, till the French consul, at the request of the beautiful Madame Sainte-Lucie, gave him shelter and smuggled him aboard the *Naïade*, just then sailing for Marseilles.

When Télémaque reached this point in his souvenirs, he took on the air of an intelligent dog who has been whipped, and hastily put the cross, the epaulettes, and the cocked-hat back in their wrappings. He looked uneasily out of the window for fear some one should have seen them from the avenue, and having replaced the precious box in the wardrobe and locked it up, he went downstairs again into the shop and poured a few drops of water into the savoury, simmering stew.

The hands of the clock which hung above the counter pointed to eleven, and a crowd of little urchins, with mops of hair in disorder and their shirts hanging out of their ragged breeches, came galloping up to the glass door in a cloud of dust. Télémaque appeared on the threshold bearing a soup-tureen full of bits of chicken and cold fried fish, all cleanly wrapped in pieces of newspaper. Miragoane gravely and attentively superintended the distribution from the doorstep agitating her tail the while.

The little folks, tumbling over each other, pressed round the negro, who in a stern nasal voice gave the order :

"Right-about face."

The children fell into line, hands down, chins up, casting longing looks at the soup-tureen.

Télémaque inspected them for some time with a serious pleasure.

"Answer to the roll," he said. "Number one, number two, number three," and handed to each one his ration. Numbers one, two, and three scampered off, with both hands hugging their portion of the titbits to their chests, and then wolfing it in a corner while they cast distrustful glances in all directions.

"Numbers four, five, six."

Number six, who had red hair, knocked down number four, who was lame, and sent his chicken bone rolling into the gutter.

Miragoane cocked her ear, Number four picked up his bone, and General Télémaque, having thus provided for his army, returned to his cooking. Perceiving that the stew was all right, he took a little wooden gun, painted red, from a drawer and called Miragoane. She came up slowly, with drooping ears and a look which meant, " Good Lord! what is the use of all this! Why complicate life needlessly. It does not give me the slightest pleasure to be drilled. But I consent to do it just to be agreeable to my master—Télémaque."

The dog stood on her hind legs, and hugged the wooden gun against her pink belly.

" Carry arms! Present arms! "

She obeyed the word of command till her legs grew tired, then she dropped on all fours again, and leaving her weapon on the tiles she gave herself a shake and went back to her place on the doorstep.

" Not well done—careless," said Télémaque. " We must begin all over again to-morrow."

But Miragoane, motionless and rigid, barked twice. Then she began to run from the doorstep to the stove, making her claws rattle on the tiles. Remi, wearing a bell-shaped straw hat of the kind used by boating-men, walked into the shop and proceeded to make himself known to Télémaque, who was too delighted to say a word. He turned his back and began to uncork a bottle of white wine.

" That you, Massa Remi? " he said at last.

"Massa Remi, son of Massa Minister, godson of my poor wife Olivette, who sold arrack, cocoanuts, and sapotillas at Port-au-Prince. Black men kill her wickedly in her shop, and drink her rum. It was printed in big letters in *Haïti Monitor*. Massa Morel-Latasse, the consul, read it to me. I was sad for Olivette, good woman. How please I am to see you, Massa Remi. Olivette not young when I marry her. They laugh at Télémaque for marrying old woman; but he know the more old a woman am, more good she cooks. Sit down, Massa Remi; dis white wine neber grow no older, 'cause we're going drink it," and he laughed long and loudly at his joke. When he had uncorked the bottle, blown away the wax round the mouth and filled the glasses, he became thoughtful and said:

"Life not last always, but death last always."

Then leaning forward he put his thick lips close to Sainte-Lucie's ear and whispered:

"I've got nice little lot of money upstairs, in a bag, to make a fine tombstone for Olivette."

After this he grew more cheerful, asked after Madame Sainte-Lucie, who was a fine woman, he said, and wanted to know what Remi was doing in Paris.

"I am studying for my degree," answered the young man with a yawn.

Télémaque did not know what degree meant, but he supposed it was something good. He half closed

his fawning eyes as he clinked glasses. Then he
asked if Remi would not be a general some day.

"It's fine," he said, with a sigh, "it's fine to be
a general, but it has its drawbacks."

"You were a general yourself once, Télémaque,"
said Remi, who found the negro amusing; "it was
under that wicked ape of a Soulouque, wasn't it?"

Télémaque looked uneasy. His thick lips trembled.

"Massa Remi, you mustn't speak like dat of the
Emperor," he stuttered.

Remi had heard his father say that the general
was horribly afraid of Soulouque, whom he imagined
to be still alive. So he added:

"Do you think his ghost will come in the night
and drag you out of bed? He has been dead these
last ten years."

The negro shook his head slowly.

"No, Massa Remi," he said.

It was no use Remi saying every one knew that
Soulouque died in Jamaica in 1867. The negro
replied:

"No, Massa Remi, the Emperor not dead, he in
hiding," and Télémaque's forehead puckered over
its hard skull.

From the copper saucepan came a pleasing odour
of meat and spices. Télémaque sniffed it and grew
cheerful again.

"Now we'll breakfast, Massa Remi," he said with
a laugh.

He laid the cloth in an arbour hung with virginia creeper; his little garden looked over fields of lettuces. The banks of the railway to Versailles barred the horizon. Remi was gazing abstractedly at this meagre country, when the negro reappeared grinning from ear to ear above the smoking dish he carried in both hands.

" It something very good, Massa Remi," he said.

Miragoane, put in charge of the shop while they ate, which they did with a good appetite, turned at intervals towards the table with a resigned expression. When they had finished the rabbit, washed down with Argenteuil wine, they lingered lovingly over an excellent Brie cheese and new bread.

"You are very comfortable here, Télémaque," said Remi, who was himself perfectly happy.

Télémaque sighed deeply, for human nature is never satisfied.

" Do you know what is wanting in my restaurant, Massa Remi? my portrait in a gilt frame. It would look so well over the counter. As I told you, I have nice sum of money upstairs in a bag, for my poor Olivette's tombstone; but I would give a fair slice of it to the painter who did my portrait."

Sainte-Lucie assured the general he should have his portrait, without touching the money meant for his godmother's mausoleum.

" I am a painter," he said to the astonished

Télémaque; "next time I come I will bring my box of colours and a canvas and make a portrait of you."

Miragoane announced the arrival of two customers, soldiers who wanted cans of beer. While Télémaque disappeared through the trap-door which shut in the stair to the cellar, Remi, whose pipe had gone out, went to the counter for a match, when who should he see going down the avenue but the little old gentleman he had caught sight of in the gilt drawing-room of the ladies in the Rue des Feuillantines, the same little old gentleman with the same white whiskers and the same umbrella.

"Télémaque, come here, quick, quick!" he cried.

The trap-door was raised, and Télémaque appeared like a subterranean but kindly genius. He laughed from the midst of the bottles of beer which he would have immediately proceeded to uncork and serve to the two waiting soldiers. But Remi caught him by his white jacket and led him, puzzled, to the threshold of the shop.

"Télémaque, do you know that old gentleman?" he asked, pointing a finger at the bent back of the worthy man.

The negro, hugging the two bottles against his chest, answered with a great peal of laughter:

"Why of course, Massa Remi; he my landlord, his name Massa Sarriette. I going to ask him to do some repair in my attic."

"Télémaque, you mustn't ask that old man to
do any repairs," said Remi; adding in a severe
voice :

" Do you pay your rent regularly, Télémaque ? "

Was it to be supposed that a restaurant-keeper
could live in the same house for twenty-one years
and not pay his rent ?

Remi then learnt that Monsieur Sarriette was
considered a rich man, that he lived most of the
time in Normandy, where he had property, and was
always measuring public monuments with his umbrella.

The enthusiastic youth exclaimed :

"Télémaque, I will paint your portrait. I will
paint you in your general's uniform, with a red
feather in your hat and four epaulettes."

"That would be beautiful, Massa Remi," said
the black man with a grave and contrite air ; " but
you mustn't do it, because it would vex the Emperor who is in hiding. You can paint me in
black dress clothes with three diamond studs in
my shirt."

Remi, who never indulged in reflections of any
kind, and was never surprised whatever happened
around and about him, caught himself wondering,
as he walked down the Avenue Saint Germain, why
he had been so excited when he saw the old friend
of the ladies in the Rue des Feuillantines go by.

CHAPTER IX

AVING meditated profoundly on the pearl-grey letter on Twelfth Night, and the rendezvous at the fountain, Branchut the moralist finished by building up an ideal conception of these mysterious events. He no longer thirsted for Sainte-Lucie's blood; in his opinion the creole had nothing whatever to do with the matter.

The philosopher arrived, by the help of his inner consciousness alone, at a knowledge of the truth about his adventure. Filled with contempt for the assertions of Remi, who openly acknowledged himself to be the author of the pearl-grey letter, Branchut was convinced with all the certainty of intuition that it was written by an exquisite and unhappy woman of a rare nature and exceptional conditions.

By a series of inductions such as only the brain of a metaphysician could be capable of, the moralist proved to himself by the clearest evidence that this woman was a Danish princess, that her name was Vranga, and that after having attired herself for the appointment at the fountain of the four bishops with ornaments of the most strangely poetical and melancholy character, she had fallen dead in her boudoir, surrounded by tropical plants, whose perfume, symbolical of her love for Branchut, was at once delicious and mortal.

As these sad and elegant facts were revealed to him, one by one, by dint of subjective enquiry and internal cogitation, he communicated them to his friend Labanne, who found nothing surprising in them. His successive discoveries on the subject of the Princess Vranga, however, had the effect of plunging Branchut into a state of melancholy eloquence.

"I must expiate by the most refined tortures," he said, "the incomparable crime of having caused the death of this unparalleled creature, who was nervous as a racehorse, and learned as Hypatia."

Grievous twitchings affected all the nerves of his expressive nose. Vranga became his one idea; he lived only in her memory. In his despair he forgot to borrow any clothes from Labanne, and in his melancholy detachment wandered about the Boulevard Saint-Michel draped in his horse-blanket as in a shroud.

"You see," he would say to his friends when they stopped to speak to him, "I am in mourning." And he would point to his head, on which was something that had a vague resemblance to crape, twisted round something that had a vague resemblance to a hat.

While he thus wore mourning for the Princess Vranga, Remi was becoming colder and colder towards the hostess of "The Famished Cat." He never ventured alone to the establishment, and would not even leave his companions to get a match from the table by the sink, where Virginie eternally rinsed glasses.

He was growing serious and painting zealously. There was another fellow now in Labanne's studio, a real hard worker, a muscular fellow as strong as a horse, who with sleeves turned up, and open shirt front showing his hairy chest, painted all day without saying a word. His peasant's face, deeply lined and coloured like the earth, garnished with a bristly beard, expressed no sentiment of any kind; his round eyes observed everything, but never gave a clue to his own thoughts. It was Potrel—Potrel of whose ingratitude Virginie was never tired of speaking. He had returned from Fontainebleau, where he had been painting for two years, and Labanne lent him a corner of his studio until the one he had taken at Montmartre should be vacant. Potrel spoke little, and badly: bending over his easel, his palette on his thumb, his eyes half shut, he would reply to all Labanne's wild theories the

P

one word "Possibly," which he articulated as he revived with an indrawn breath the expiring ashes in the blackened bowl of his pipe. One day Labanne said to him:

"The absolute is unrealisable; no artist can express absolute beauty."

"Possibly," answered Potrel, and went on painting. He hired a model, an admirable little Italian, snivelling and cunning, who stole his tobacco, so Sainte-Lucie could now try his hand at "academies."

When Potrel got off his stool to stretch his legs, he would give Remi a few brief but clear words of advice and resume his work.

One morning, when he was scratching his beard and biting his nails, Remi asked him how it was he was not working. Potrel pointed with his hand in the direction of the skylight, and said:

"That cursed gewgaw there prevents my painting."

The "cursed gewgaw" was no other than the sun, just then filling the studio with blinding light.

Potrel had a huge appetite which he satisfied in cabmen's restaurants. When Remi spoke to him of "The Famished Cat," he would simply smile. One day, however, he asked if Virginie had kept her fine figure. After many vain attempts Remi succeeded in enticing him one evening to the establishment in the Rue Saint-Jacques. Virginie, red as a peony, brought him a large slice of ham.

"Eat it, Monsieur Potrel," she said. "It is very good, very delicate. See how white the fat is. You are not drinking anything. Try this beer; I bottled it last month. You used to be fond of beer."

And Potrel ate and drank, while Virginie, standing behind his chair, her face illuminated with a seraphic smile, gasped ecstatically at every mouthful the silent and robust man swallowed.

The hostess did not even notice when Remi left the tavern, and he gave a sigh of relief, like a man who has been eased from an oppressive weight.

On his way home he met the concierge of the house where the two ladies lived going into the wine shop, and a little farther on he saw the man's wife gossiping with the greengrocer. Then an idea suddenly occurred to him. He walked into the deserted lodge, and looked about to see if he could discover the name of the ladies on the fourth storey. Above one of the little pigeon-holes were the words "Madame Lourmel, rentière."

Next day he saw from the window Mademoiselle Lourmel giving her birds water in a small china cup. He watched her involuntarily with a warm and lively sympathy. She saw him, but it was only slowly that she turned aside her frank ingenuous gaze. He noticed that she was no longer a child, and that she was very pretty.

He went at this period several times a week to Courbevoie, and the portrait of Télémaque emerged little by little from the canvas. It was a very bad portrait, but Télémaque was enchanted with it. When the shop was shut at night, he would prop the painting up on a table between two lighted candles, and dance the Calenda before it, or else sing to it in a soft nasal voice:

> " Canga-do-ki-la,
> Canga-li."

Miragoane, seated on her haunches, gravely took part in the ceremonies. One day she affectionately licked the nose of the portrait: the paint was wet, but the damage done was easily repaired.

Télémaque had moments of regret that Olivette was not on the canvas beside him, dressed in her red shawl. It did not deeply distress him, however, and he continued to dance the Calenda.

CHAPTER X

EMI got up one morning with the pleasant thought in his mind, that he had finished the negro's portrait, and that it was in its way a remarkable work. He could see, framed in the window opposite his, two little hands tapping on the keys of a piano; they were no longer red, and did not tap so hard. He also noticed that the chandelier was imprisoned in a muslin bag, and that there was a great deal of bustling about in the ordinarily calm apartment.

The little hands shut down the piano-lid and disappeared, to reappear carrying leather bags and hat-boxes. Remi, who felt that something of importance was happening, stuck to his post of observation, and kept his eye on the approaches to the house. After two hours' watching he saw the porter come down carrying a pyramid of trunks and boxes; a cab stopped at the door, and he saw Madame Lourmel's servant pile still more travelling bags and boxes in it. Remi seized his paint-box, emptied all the money he had in his secretary into his pocket, and rushed bare-headed, in a jersey and his slippers, downstairs and into the street. He hailed the astonished driver of a passing cab and hurried him in pursuit of the vehicle which had just moved off under its tottering pyramid of luggage, and into which he had seen the skirts of a dress disappearing.

The two cabs crossed Paris, one behind the other, and drew up in the courtyard of the St. Lazare railway station. Remi followed the two ladies, and, still in his unconventional attire, climbed the stairs. Mademoiselle Lourmel turned her head to see this strange traveller, whom she recognised perfectly well. Her look showed a surprise which included amusement, and something of admiration. As he stood by Madame Lourmel at the ticket-office and heard her ask for two tickets for Avranches, he breathed a sigh of relief and also took a ticket for Avranches. Madame Lourmel went off with her daughter to register the luggage, and Remi, who had no formality of that kind to fulfil, decided to do a little useful shopping. He ran to a ready-made clothes-store in the Rue de la Pepinière, bought two or three suits without looking at them, and paid the shopkeeper, who had half a mind to have his extraordinary customer arrested. Suddenly Remi gave a cry of despair:

"Shoes!" he said; "shoes!"

The shopkeeper, a handsome Jew with a goat-like head, an amiable mouth and pitiless eyes, replied coldly that " he didn't keep the article."

" Give me yours, then," said the desperate creole.

But the Israelite, who was becoming more and more uneasy, looked so forbidding that Remi went off in his slippers, putting on some of the new clothes as he went along through the bustle of the garish street. He stopped to snatch a hat hanging outside a shop, and flung down the money for it. It was twenty-seven minutes past four already. Remi tore along towards the station, and by thirty-two minutes past he was in the waiting-room, which had probably never before been entered by a traveller in slippers. A pair of violet eyes welcomed him as he entered and seemed to say :

"We were waiting for you. You are very extraordinary with your brown skin, your new clothes put on all awry, and your bedroom slippers. But we are not in the least afraid of you or annoyed at you; you don't look at all ill-tempered, and you have a bold air which is rather pleasing. This is all we have to say to you. If you want to know anything more you must ask mamma."

If the daughter's eyes talked after this fashion, Madame de Lourmel's glance betrayed that sort of uneasiness noticeable in a hen when one coaxes her chickens from her with bread crumbs.

Remi left mother and daughter discreetly alone in their carriage, and settled himself at the other end of the train. Having taken his seat, the first question he asked himself was when, where, and how could he get some shoes; then, on counting his money, he found he had twenty-one francs thirty-five centimes left, and felt quite reassured. His second question was, if by any chance he was in love with Mademoiselle Lourmel.

CHAPTER XI

BOUT a week after Remi's departure, Monsieur Godet-Laterrasse was seized with an ardent desire to see him. With a volume of Tacitus in his pocket, he went off to the Rue des Feuillantines, where he learnt that his pupil had disappeared.

A cloud crossed his noble brow, that brow which, if it had been a mirror, would only have reflected the sky, the gulls of the Pacific, and the constellations of the two hemispheres. People with superior minds are more given to presentiment than ordinary beings. Godet-Laterrasse had a presentiment. That is why, laying aside their old enmity, he went to see Labanne in his studio.

The sculptor, who had no idea of time or space, could tell him nothing. He took him to interview the opulent Virginie, who attributed Remi's flight to a secret sorrow, the nature of which she left unexplained; but she insinuated that she had not failed to anticipate this eventuality. If, as she feared, it was love which had driven Monsieur Sainte-Lucie to despair,

she was truly grieved, but one could not please every-
body, unless one was the sort of woman which is
unfortunately too numerous in these days. She had
done nothing to make Monsieur Remi jealous of
Monsieur Potrel ; she was an honest woman and had
nothing to reproach herself with. She appealed to
the picture of " The Famished Cat " to bear witness
to her innocence, and returned to the dark corner,
where she spent most of her time washing glasses.

With a mind full of care, Godet-Laterrasse returned to the heights of Montmartre. He came
down again next day on the top of an omnibus and
revisited the studio, which he had chosen as his
centre of operations. There he found Branchut,
who, in his horse-blanket, was occupied in writing
a treatise on love. Full of his subject, Branchut
proceeded to expound it.

"Love," he said, " can only be absolute between
two beings who have never seen each other. Eternal
absence is necessary for two souls to be in perfect
harmony. Solitude is the condition necessary to
the growth of a definite passion."

Godet-Laterrasse resisted the temptations to an
oratorical duel on these sublime heights, and asked
the moralist if he had seen Sainte-Lucie.

Branchut was totally ignorant of the creole's
disappearance, but a sudden intuition enabled him
to explain it. In the twinkling of an eye many

things were revealed to him. According to him, this disappearance had a not remote connection with the death of the Princess Vranga. Sainte-Lucie's gloomy behaviour, in the circumstances that preceded and accompanied the lamentable and poetic end of the Princess Vranga, was due, in the moralist's eyes, to an eternal remorse that had taken possession of the soul of this young man, frivolous in appearance, but Machiavellian in reality.

"Princess Vranga had to die," said the philosopher serenely. "It was needful for her to die, so that the love she felt for me might be realised in the absolute. Sainte-Lucie's crime has probably led him to suicide; he intercepted, over and over again, the letters the Princess had written to me, the text of which I have reconstructed from intuition! and with satanic irony he gave me only the last one."

So said Branchut, whose nose twitched in his livid face touched with spots of colour, and whose eyes were haggard and bloodshot. Labanne arrived just in time to drag the unfortunate tutor out into the street, wildly shaking his umbrella above his head.

"My poor moralist!" said he, "he has never had finer ideas than he has now. A grain of phosphorus in the brain makes a man of genius;

unhappily he has two grains, that's the misfortune ! "

Labanne remembered having heard Sainte-Lucie
speak enthusiastically of a black general who kept
a restaurant at Courbevoie ; the sculptor thought
he might know something.   Any way, he would like
to see the negro himself.

They got on top of a tram, which took them to
the Place de l'Étoile, where Labanne instinctively
stopped at the first café, and, having ordered sundry
bottles of beer, lost himself in interminable chatter.
Monsieur Godet-Laterrasse answered him at great
length, and though Labanne did not listen to him,
he continued to talk.   Many fine theories were
aired.   All of a sudden the sculptor made a gesture
in the air with his thumb, and said :

"It would be quite possible to make that thing
bearable to the eye."

"That thing" was the Arc de Triomphe.

"It would be simple, but you'll see no one will
think of it.   One need only establish a sufficient
number of stalls at the foot of the edifice, and
let them to cobblers, public letter-writers, and fried-
potato sellers, especially the latter, because of the
smoke.   These stalls ought to be sordid, with in-
correct, vulgarly-painted signs.   The builders might
be allowed to take stone from the monument itself,
particularly at the corners ; this would soften down

the harsh outline. It would be desirable to fill up
the holes resulting from these various depredations
with a few spadefuls of earth, and plant beech-nuts
and acorns. The beeches and oaks would spread
out their green branches at different heights, and
so break the monotony of the grey surface; their
roots, pushing down into the masonry, would cause
most picturesque cracks. There would have to be
a lot of ivy, but that tenacious plant would not
fail us; it thrives on stonework. The wind and
the birds would sow seeds of gilli-flowers, which
love old walls, and a thousand other things in the
dusty orifices. Saxifrage, eager for moisture, black-
berries, and virginia creeper would spring up and
multiply at random. The top of the edifice would
be honeycombed with pigeons' nests; the swallows
would plaster theirs under the vaulting; troops of
crows, attracted by the dead dormice and field mice,
would swoop down at nightfall. Thus, the Arc
de Triomphe, if kept up with some sort of intelligent care, would be looked at by poets, copied
by painters, and considered as a work of art.
Waiter, another *bock*."

Night was falling. The artist and the thinker
decided that they would not go any further, so they
took the tram back to Montparnasse.

CHAPTER XII

ADAME LOURMEL and her daughter settled themselves in a little stone house with a thatched roof at a small unfrequented seaside place, a few miles from Avranches.

Remi, happy and intoxicated with the salt air, went off with his paint-box to a neighbouring fair. He had only fourteen francs seventy centimes left, but he had a pair of shoes.

Lines of carts were drawn up on the outskirts of the market-place. Under the trees there was a great assembly of red faces, fringed with fair beards, the rumps of calves plastered with dung, horned cattle, pink muzzles, shining haunches, and white caps. The squealing of pigs being taken out of carts was heard above every other sound of man or beast. Women, with cotton fichus and gold chains round their necks, stood stolidly in their straight skirts by the waggons, keenly watching over them, while the men, in full-plaited blue blouses, did business over a pot of cider in some *cabaret* full of flies.

Remi passed under the holly branch above the door, and sat down at one of the tables with his pencil and paper. He made a sketch of a peasant, then another and another, then one of a group of peasants who were watching him. He said he would do the portrait of any one of them for a franc; but this offer did not loosen their purse-strings. "Go and get your sweethearts," he said; "I will draw them."

There was a murmur in the crowd, and three or four particularly jovial fellows pushed a bouncing girl in front of Remi. She was purple, almost violet, and she was laughing from ear to ear. Remi made a sketch of her, in which she could be recognised by her cap and her cross.

One of the jovial fellows pulled a franc out of a woollen stocking and handed it to the painter, then, neatly folding the picture in four, he tucked it under his smock.

The general opinion was that the Parisian could make a good likeness, and Remi went back with several pieces of silver in his pocket. He slept in the most rustic inn in the village, where Madame Lourmel had taken up her quarters, and appeared next day on the dazzling beach, where the striped bathing machines were drawn up in line.

The sea, blue on the horizon, was coming in slowly, breaking on the sand in oily green waves edged with foam. A soft damp sky, one of those treacherous skies which both caress and scorch the tender skins of city dwellers, arched in the round horizon. Skinny women in bathing costumes, their hair in water-proof caps, were scurrying before the incoming waves. He saw Mademoiselle Lourmel; she was wearing a fluttering violet veil.

He wanted to throw his arms round her neck; but he caught sight of Monsieur Sarriette, with the same white whiskers and the same umbrella, coming down a little path to the shore.

"Good morning, Monsieur Sarriette," he said to the astonished old man.

At the end of a quarter of an hour they were great friends.

"I am very fond of old monuments," said Monsieur Sarriette, "and, believe me or not, I spent three weeks measuring all the walls of the Abbey on Saint-Michael's Mount. I have a way of my own of taking measurements—I use my umbrella. The average height of the Abbey ramparts is seventy-two umbrellas, and in the church the pillars of the nave measure no less than thirty-seven umbrellas, three handles, and two ferrules."

Monsieur Sarriette was delighted to hear that Remi was a painter. They arranged to explore the whole countryside together; Remi was to make sketches and Monsieur Sarriette was to measure the historical buildings.

" Present me to Madame Lourmel," said Remi.

"Monsieur Remi Sainte-Lucie, son of Monsieur Sainte-Lucie, a former Minister of Haïti," said the good man at this request.

Remi bowed low first to Madame Lourmel, who was dumb with astonishment, then to the girl, who opened her violet eyes widely and smiled with her flower-like mouth.

That evening Madame Lourmel and her daughter leaned at their window breathing the salt air and watching the moon rise over the sparkling sea.

"But, my dear child," said Madame Lourmel, " we know nothing about his family, or his fortune, or his mode of life."

"But, mamma, I love him," answered the girl, with the audacity of innocence.

" What do you mean, Jeanne ?   You know nothing about him," said the mother.

And Jeanne, whose beautiful eyes were shining with a slightly rebellious tenderness, answered :

"Perhaps I don't know him, but I know him again."

CHAPTER XIII

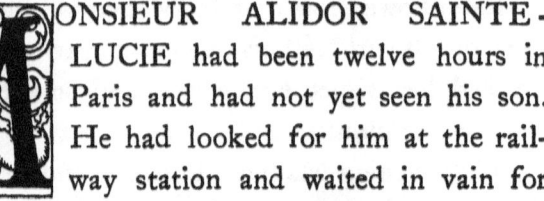ONSIEUR ALIDOR SAINTE-
LUCIE had been twelve hours in
Paris and had not yet seen his son.
He had looked for him at the railway station and waited in vain for
him at the hotel. Remi's absence irritated him, his
nerves were shaken by his long voyage, and in the
peaceful bed at the hotel he could still feel the
rolling of the ship and the oscillation of the express
train. He awoke in a bad humour; the vague
uneasiness of his limbs spread to his brain.

Lying back in a cab, jolted by the rough paving
of the streets leading up to Montmartre, he thought
with dissatisfaction of his son's education. Godet-
Laterrasse did not appear to have troubled himself
much about it. Four years had gone by and Remi
had not taken his bachelor's degree. It was for
such a result as this that he had chosen a poor but
superior man as tutor. He had expected better
things of Godet-Laterrasse, who spoke so eloquently
and so austerely in political cafés.

The letters the man wrote him annoyed him;

they were so indefinite and so hollow. He was furthermore furious with Remi for not coming to the station to embrace him as he should have done. The smell of fried fish rose to his nostrils exasperatingly. The cab went slowly, drawn by a lean horse which, with a hanging head and a long tongue, offered its crupper to the whip. At last the cabman stopped without saying a word, and the hundred and sixty steps of the Passage Cotin rose steeply before the cab door. Monsieur Alidor, having alighted, handed the man a five-franc piece. The latter, pimply faced, huge and covered with dust, put it between his teeth without a word of explanation. Then followed a long mute comedy; the cabman turned his colossal body slowly on the seat, while he dived into one of his pockets from which he drew a bag. Then he stopped to survey his horse which shook convulsively, explored another pocket, urged his horse several paces forward to get out of the way of a waggon, from which there was not the slightest danger. Finally, he produced seven sous from the depths of his red waistcoat, and proffered them to his exasperated fare. It was all the change he had. Monsieur Alidor turned his back on him in a raging temper, and he drove away, grumbling and plying his whip.

The mulatto's irreproachable patent shoes cracked on the disjointed stones of the Passage Cotin as they

climbed step by step the arduous way, which even
in mid-summer was noxious and greasy. At length,
after slipping upon the viscous steps of the interior
staircase, Monsieur Alidor tugged viciously at the
deer's foot, which served as a bell-pull at the
mouldy doorway. After waiting several minutes
the door opened cautiously, and a head, enveloped
in a multi-coloured handkerchief, peeped out. The
superior man, aroused from a profound sleep, had
only had time to slip into a pair of trousers spat-
tered all over with mud of long standing. The
room smelt of damp tobacco ; a greenish light, nearly
exhausted by the numerous indirect channels it tra-
versed painfully, filtered through the dirty window.
Political caricatures were pinned on the walls, the
washing-stand was covered with tattered, unbound
volumes, and a piece of soap, a comb, and half a roll
of bread lay among the manuscripts and dictionaries
on the writing-table. These things spoke so plainly
of habits of sloth and disorder, that after one
glance round the room, Sainte-Lucie felt he knew
the tutor as well as if he had followed him from café
to café for twenty years. The unfortunate creole
tried to make up for the ignominy of his dwelling
by the extreme dignity of his bearing.

"Excuse me," he said to the former, minister,
"for receiving you in the disordered cell of a
modern anchorite." Then he added, drawing him-

self up, " We are the Benedictines of the nineteenth century." And he tried to smuggle into his pockets the combs and the crusts of bread which disfigured the table.

Sainte-Lucie had the sense to recognise that he had deceived himself, but had not been deceived. For the matter of that, how could Monsieur Godet-Laterrasse deceive any one? The poor, little, dirty lizard of a man was pitiful to behold, but if there was one sentiment foreign to Sainte-Lucie's soul, it was pity. And that he had only himself to blame, made him the less forgiving to the innocent tutor. In his anger he bit his lips, and his eyes grew sombre, but it pleased him for the moment to dissimulate. His gentle voice took on an accent which was almost caressing as he said :

" My dear Godet, forgive me for having surprised you in your bed " (here he threw a terrible glance at the object he politely named *a bed*). " You are the first person I have called on. We will go now and surprise Remi. I wrote to tell him of my arrival, but he did not trouble himself to meet me. I'll pull his ears for him."

At these words a shiver of terror shook the frame of the tutor, who however far he threw his head back still looked up into the tall mulatto's enigmatical face.

He tried to smile, and stammered out something

about having given Remi a holiday for the day, and
that he had no doubt gone into the country with his
friends. The wretched man thus gained a day's
respite; he spent it in researches which only tired
him without resulting in any discovery.

By eight o'clock the next morning Monsieur
Sainte-Lucie was again in the anchorite's cell, which
the Benedictine of the nineteenth century had tidied
up a little. He himself wore a white necktie, and
that stoical expression which rendered him so
remarkable on ceremonial occasions. It was not
only fear of Soulouque's former minister which
troubled him. He had but small credit in
Bather's Alley, and as he did not possess a franc
in the world he was in a fix. The two hundred
francs which the consul of Haïti remitted to him
regularly every month went mostly in paying old
debts to various tradesmen, for he was honest;
what remained never lasted long. He loved to
throw money about, and now he did not possess a
franc. His misery, as he followed Sainte-Lucie,
was so excessive it blinded him, made him giddy
and little by little indifferent as to what might
happen. The mulatto's voice ordering the cabman
to drive to the Rue des Feuillantines brought him
to his senses, and he endeavoured to postpone the
climax for a few hours.

"Dear sir," he said, "we shall be more likely

to find Remi in the afternoon, at the time for our lessons."

The sly, suspicious Sainte-Lucie felt that something was being hidden from him, but it afforded him a kind of pleasure to pile up grievances in his memory, so he replied with perfect good nature :

"Very well ; we will go to breakfast. You must be hungry, Monsieur Godet."

They breakfasted in a café on the boulevard. The tutor ate little, and fearfully watched his huge companion devouring the mass of food that his bulk demanded. The man had never seemed to him so broad and so tall. Enormous muscular bronze arms were visible through the Haïtian's cuffs with their gold links. He talked in a voice which was almost childishly gentle, and the twinkling of his cruel eyes was softened by the lashes he lowered so trustingly. And that trustfulness added to the tutor's anguish.

The breakfast dragged on to liqueurs and cigars, but finish it did at last; then a waiter called a cab, and parent and tutor started for the Rue des Feuillantines.

Nothing but a miracle could save him now, and Godet half expected, by the intervention of Providence, to find Remi in his room, " digging away at Tacitus."

The landlady of the hotel dashed his hopes to
the ground with her first word.

"Monsieur Remi has not come back," she said;
"you ought to inform the police."

Monsieur Alidor folded his arms and turned
towards the tutor. The colour of his face was
unchanged, but his lips were white and his eyes
bloodshot.

"Where is he?" he hissed through his closed
teeth. "You are responsible for him."

He stretched out his powerful hand and grasped
the tutor's arm, who, as the earth did not open
beneath him, flung back his head and contemplated
the staircase. Even in his downfall he was sublime.
Sainte-Lucie, looking round, saw rows of brass
candlesticks on a shelf, beneath which hung keys
each bearing a numbered tag and a spirit merchant's advertisement. These things bore witness
to European civilisation. Had he instead of them
seen a sandy plain, the abrupt sides of a deep
ravine, or the palm-trees of his native island, he
would in all probability have given way to his
desire to strangle the tutor. He abstained from
so doing, out of respect for European manners,
and contented himself with saying:

"I shall not leave you until you have found him."

Then began a series of drives in cabs to such
places as Godet-Laterrasse could suggest. He

dined with the mulatto in sumptuous restaurants, ate of succulent dishes, and received the obsequious smiles of waiters. In the evening he mounted the thickly carpeted staircase of Sainte-Lucie's hotel, the inordinately elongated shadow of his inevitable companion mounting by his side. He was shown into a fine bedroom, and heard the key turn in the lock behind him. When the door opened next morning, it would be for him to resume his life of painful splendour.

There was always a cab waiting for them in the street, which took them on an unceasing round the whole day through. They drove to "The Famished Cat," where Virginie assured the father of the lively interest she took in his son.

She had often mended Monsieur Remi's linen, she said. She would have gone to the stake for him. She was not like so many women one sees about. " Go and look in the Morgue," she added with a sigh.

She dived into her kitchen, and reappeared a moment later, her eyes screwed up and her nose red, and in her hand a bill which Monsieur Remi had not settled.

She profited too by the occasion to remind Monsieur Godet that he also owed her for sundry *bocks*. But the man of iron had forgotten his purse. Besides, he had given up the struggle; his ambulatory prison exhausted him. He was dragged from "The Famished Cat" to Labanne's studio. The sculptor stroked his ruddy beard and declared that he did not as yet "see" the expiatory monument to the Victims of Tyranny, but that he was studying the flora of the Antilles. He showed Monsieur Sainte-Lucie an easel, already half buried under a pile of books.

"That was Remi's easel," he said; "the young scoundrel was beginning to paint as dexterously as a monkey."

"Is my son a painter?" exclaimed Sainte-Lucie.

Then with a gesture which was now familiar to him, he hoisted the tutor into the cab which was waiting.

They went to the prefecture of police; they went to see Dion, who was busy writing a poem. On the wall hung a pair of crossed foils, and a death's-head, wearing a mask fringed with lace, ornamented his bookcase.

They went to see Mercier, who was living with a high-coloured, formidably built dame—a *sage-femme* by profession.

They explored the deepest depths of Batignolles till they found Potrel painting in his studio. They went to see a young lady called Marie, and a young lady called Louise, who were very playful with the former minister and called him "papa." One day, after an extra good breakfast, Godet-Laterrasse, seeing the cab already waiting to carry him off, asked if he might at least be allowed to go to his apartment to get a clean shirt and some socks. Sainte-Lucie, without answering him, ordered the cabman to stop at the first hosier's he came to.

That same day they went to visit Télémaque. It was the first time that Miragoane had seen a cab stop at her master's door, and she greeted it by barking furiously. When Télémaque saw Soulouque's former minister get out of it, he was seized with respect and terror.

"That you, Massa Sainte-Lucie?" were the only words he could say, though his mouth remained open, and he cast furtive glances towards the cab, fearful lest the Emperor himself should be hidden in it. Once reassured on this point, he smiled widely at Monsieur Godet-Laterrasse, and went down into the cellar in search of bottled beer.

During his absence Sainte-Lucie examined the portrait, which in its gilded frame hung over the counter.

"Isn't it fine, massa? isn't it really beautiful?" said the negro, his head appearing above the trapdoor, on a level with the floor. "It is your son, massa, who painted it. Massa Remi, he is a sorcerer."

The father turned two venomous eyes towards the tutor and said nothing.

When Télémaque learned from the former minister of Remi's disappearance, he pondered for a long time. His half-closed eyes, like those of a cat dropping off to sleep, seemed to interrogate those of Miragoane. Finally he shook his head, and said with religious gravity:

"Massa, it is love which has carried away the young man. Young men are moved by love, and agitated, as Brother Voodoo is agitated when he dances on the serpent's cage. There is something good about an old woman who knows how to cook: but there is something good, too, about a pretty young girl."

Here Télémaque held his peace.

"Do you know where my son is?" asked Monsieur Sainte-Lucie.

"Yes, massa," replied Télémaque; "he is where the young lady is."

When he was asked where was the young lady of whom he spoke, he replied, with an infantine smile:

"I don't know, massa."

And nothing more could be got out of him, so Sainte-Lucie bundled the tutor with his packet of shirts and socks back into the cab, and conjured Télémaque to let him know anything he could find out about Remi.

CHAPTER XIV

ÉLÉMAQUE was dressed in his best black clothes, in which he looked so respectable that the waiter at the hotel unhesitatingly showed him up the main staircase.

"Good morning, massa," he said to Monsieur Alidor, whom he found arrayed in a pink sleeping suit. "I know where Massa Remi is; he where the young lady is, and the young lady is at the seaside, at Avranches."

He then explained that, having several times noticed the young man was much interested in Monsieur Sarriette, his landlord at Courbevoie, he thought that perhaps it might be because of something to do with a young lady. The butcher's wife and the baker's wife had both told him that Monsieur Sarriette, who received few visitors, was the guardian of a girl who had lost her father, and lived with her mother in the Rue des Feuillantines. Every one said the young lady was very pretty. Hearing further that Monsieur Sarriette had gone to join his ward at a little

village near Avranches, Télémaque felt quite sure
that Massa Remi had gone to Avranches too.
He declared that Brother Joseph the prophet
could not have divined things better, even though
he had first danced on his serpent's cage.

Monsieur Sainte-Lucie went at once to fetch
the tutor from his prison. He was beginning to
get used to his well-fed and stupefying life, and
merely looked at the ceiling with the air of a
poodle and a martyr, which he could so affectingly
assume when, with cruel irony, he was ordered
to pack his trunks. A waiter was sent out to
buy him some handkerchiefs, and soon, seated
beside the mulatto, he was in the train going
to Normandy. The two travellers spent the
night at Avranches.

The next day, while the morning sun shone
on the bay, turning its sands to silver, and showing up the brown crenellated buildings on Saint
Michael's Mount, Sainte-Lucie dragged Godet-
Laterrasse to the omnibus which was to take
them to the little bathing-place. He took his
place in the *coupé*, and put his prisoner under
the tilt, where he was squeezed between two
packing-cases, the corners of which stuck into his
sides. As soon as they reached the village, Sainte-
Lucie locked his victim up in a bedroom in the
hotel.

The landlady of the inn, being interrogated, told him that Monsieur Remi with his paint-box, accompanied by Monsieur Sarriette, had gone to the cliffs, and there, sure enough, after a ten minutes' walk, Monsieur Alidor found his son tranquilly sketching the rocks. The father wanted to beat him with his walking-stick, and at the same time hug him to his heart. He was still undecided which desire to satisfy when Remi saw him, and, springing up, threw his arms round his neck.

He was no longer the great sulky boy whom his father had left four years ago; he was a robust, well-grown young fellow, good-humoured and wide awake, with an honest, smiling face.

"How glad I am that you have come, papa," he said. "I was just going to write to you. This is Monsieur Sarriette—let me present him to you; he will introduce you to Madame and Madamoiselle Lourmel."

Monsieur Sarriette left off measuring the cliff with his umbrella and bowed.

That evening, beneath an innumerable cohort of stars, Monsieur Alidor Sainte-Lucie, adorned with all his creole airs and graces, offered his arm to Madame Lourmel, and led her for a stroll along the beach.

Remi walked by the side of Jeanne, and noted

the blue shadows her long lashes cast on her rounded cheeks. She raised her eyes, cool as violets steeped in dew, to the young man, and a ray of moonlight shone on her pretty teeth, as she said:

"Mamma could not understand—she could not understand a bit—why you should travel in the same train with us, without a hat, too, and in your slippers and jersey. But I knew quite well that it was because you wanted to marry me."

When Monsieur Alidor found himself alone with his son, he said in a half-scolding, half-tender tone:

"She is a very nice girl. You don't deserve such a nice girl. It was wrong of me not to tell Madame Lourmel the kind of life you have been leading in Paris, you young scamp. Well, anyhow, do you think you know how to paint?"

Then all of a sudden he struck his forehead.

"I have left that fool of a Godet locked up all this time in his room!" he cried.

THE END